TROUBLE NEXT DOOR

TROUBLE NEXT DOOR

STEFANIE LONDON

Entangled Publishing, LLC
2614 South Timberline Road
Suite 105, PMB 159
Fort Collins, CO 80525
Visit our website at www.entangledpublishing.com.

Lovestruck is an imprint of Entangled Publishing, LLC.

Edited by Alycia Tornetta
Cover design by Erin Dameron-Hill
Cover art from DepositPhotos

Manufactured in the United States of America

First Edition November 2017

To every person who finds delight in makeup. Keep on shining!

Chapter One

McKenna Prescott stared at the invoice on her phone, her eyes narrowed at the Real Skin Whoppers eight-inch vibrator, and had two questions. One, was there such a thing as too much veining on a vibrator? And two, why would they name it after a hamburger?

Hungry Jack's associations aside, it didn't look half bad. It certainly had a little extra length on her previous model… but she couldn't really blame her ex for that. He could only make do with what God had given him.

You're just angry because you didn't pull the pin first. But you've learned your lesson—no more guys for the foreseeable future. It's time to focus on you.

McKenna was engaging in what she'd decided to call Operation Self-Love. There was no point crying over douchebags. Two nights ago that had been hammered home for good. Her eye makeup had been on point—a smoky dark sapphire blue with glitter and the most kick-butt set of false lashes ever—but by the time she'd come home she looked like Britney Spears circa 2007. Total hot-mess meltdown.

And to think she'd worn blue because she knew Gage loved it and then he'd gone and tossed it back in her face by saying he wanted a classy, elegant woman on his arm. Like she was trash because she liked shiny things.

Ugh, Gage. He wasn't the man of her dreams, by any means. But he'd impressed her parents and given her a brief taste of their approval. His rejection last night hadn't hurt her heart the way it should have, but it *had* shown her that she'd been setting the bar so low that she barely had to lift her foot to step over it. And then, once again, she'd failed. Failed to hang on to a man like Gage, failed to be impressive enough that he would want her by his side for the next step in his career.

But what about the next step in *her* career?

Screw Gage. Screw all men, actually. And screw her family, too.

McKenna was sick of being the sore point in people's lives. She was sick of choosing men who treated her like a disposable makeup wipe. It was time she started living for herself. This was the last time she was *ever* going to waste mascara on a man.

McKenna cringed as she glanced at the empty bottle of Red Hill Pinot Noir she'd consumed last night sitting on her desk. It was a fancy wine. A gift from her parents after they had visited a friend's vineyard. Probably *not* intended for wallowing in post-breakup pity while drunkenly shopping for sex toys. But it certainly explained the eye-bulging total amount of her order. Three hundred bucks wasn't too much, was it? Who the hell cared? At this point, her browser knew more about her life than any man who'd drifted in or out in the last few years. So, she was going exclusive. She could be in a committed relationship with her laptop…and Mr. Whopper, as she'd decided to call him.

Unfortunately, the drain on her credit card wasn't her

biggest worry. It was the email saying her package had been delivered even though she hadn't received a notification from the building's concierge. Those guys were like clockwork when something arrived.

How strange.

McKenna grabbed her keys and decided to go investigate. If she was going to spend Friday night alone, wallowing in her newly single status—*again*—then she may as well have a battery-operated friend.

She headed downstairs and caught the attention of the person manning the concierge desk. A small trolley behind him was piled high with packages, which meant the mail had definitely been delivered today.

"Ms. Prescott." The gentleman beamed. "How can I help you?"

This was the one time she hated the fact that the guy somehow managed to remember *everyone's* name and what floor they lived on. A little anonymity would *not* have gone astray on this occasion.

"I'm trying to find a missing parcel. According to the tracking information, it arrived today." McKenna frowned. "It's, uh, quite a...valuable parcel."

God, of all the bloody packages to go missing...

She scanned the email with the tracking information, then told him, "It says it was delivered at three forty-two p.m."

"I'm sorry," the older man said, scratching his head. "I haven't had anything arrive for you and I've logged all the packages that came in today. Nothing had your apartment number on it."

The universe must have her name on a hit list somewhere. Who up there had she pissed off so royally? Not only could she not keep a guy around for more than five minutes, but she was also destined not to have an artificial replacement, either.

She braced her hands on the concierge's desk and leaned

forward, giving him her most charming smile. "Please, Matthew. If you could do some digging, I'd *really* appreciate it."

"Let me look up the freight company." He tapped at the computer screen. "We had three parcels come in from them today. Delivered at three forty-two p.m."

"That's the right time."

"They were logged under apartment 601, 312, and 110." He cocked his head. "You're on level one, right? What apartment number, again?"

"101," McKenna said, a sinking feeling settling into the pit of her stomach.

"What name was on the parcel? Yours?"

She cringed. "Noelle Smith."

It was her alias for any time she didn't want to give her real name out—like if a creepy dude wanted her number... or if she happened to be ordering several hundred dollars' worth of sex toys online. If the box gave anything away, she could claim ignorance and blame it on her "friend," Noelle.

"It's a gift for a girlfriend," she added, meekly.

"Looks like it was logged under apartment 110. The shipping company must have gotten the address wrong."

McKenna checked her email with the shipping confirmation. *Shit.* Looks like *she* was the one who got the address wrong—clearly, drunk typing was not her forte. Great, now she'd have to convince him that it was her parcel... and that meant showing him the invoice with all her dirty little secrets in black-and-white print.

"Uh, actually, looks like that was my fault." She put on her best sheepish expression. "I typed the number in wrong. Fat fingers, I guess."

Matthew nodded. "It happens."

"If I show you the invoice will you still let me have it? I know it doesn't have my name on it, but I have proof of purchase." McKenna sucked in a breath when he frowned. "I really need my parcel."

"I'm afraid that's out of my control, Ms. Prescott. 110 already picked it up."

Double shit. Can this day get any more embarrassing?

"Looks like I'll have to go knock on their door then." And hope to God that they hadn't opened her parcel. "Who's in 110, again?"

She tried to think. Who was on her floor? There was the sweet older couple with the adorable terrier who always wore a tartan coat. They weren't at 110, she was sure of it. Then, there was a father and daughter a few doors down, a guy who only seemed to be around a week or so everything month. And…

Triple shit.

She knew *exactly* who was in 110. The only guy in the building who'd ever made her look twice—Mr. tall, blond, and handsome who had an equally tall, blond, and gorgeous girlfriend. Or was she his wife? She'd only bumped into him a few times and he'd always had this broody, far-away look about him like his brain was operating on some other level. On the few occasions she'd said hello, he had done little more than grunt a barely passable return greeting.

Not him. Please, anyone but him.

"Beckett Walsh," the concierge said.

Of course it was him. The universe was not going to cut her a break today. As if it wasn't bad enough that her ex had dropped by her work today to "check that she was coping" after their breakup two nights ago—seriously, who *did* that?—and she'd had to play nice because her area manager was visiting, when all she'd wanted to do was grab Gage's face and mush it into the lipstick rack.

"Thanks for your help," McKenna said.

She headed toward the elevators, her shoulders slumping.

Maybe she should cut her losses and move to the outback where she could live as a hermit. It wouldn't be all bad. She could adopt a dingo and be some kind of local urban legend. The girl who turned her back on a box of vibrators.

Ugh. Three hundred bucks wasn't that much…was it? On a retail wage, it was. A few freelance jobs would help her make it up, but work was hard to come by at this time of year. Late July was miserable in Melbourne, oscillating between windy and cold, and rainy and colder. Not exactly peak bridal season. And the school formal calendar wouldn't kick in for months. Not to mention they were in the public holiday dead zone.

Yeah, and your hopes of giving up shitty retail work to be a real *makeup artist will be all for nothing if you keep it up.*

This was what she got for "wasting money on frivolous things," as her mother had once said to her. Maybe she wasn't entitled to sexual pleasure.

McKenna stepped into the elevator and jabbed at the button for the first floor, tapping her chunky black boot. Screw it, she'd go to apartment 110 and claim back her box of debauchery. Then she could start hunting for a new place to live.

The elevator *pinged* and she strode down the hallway, deciding not to go home first for fear of chickening out. When she got to apartment 110, she stood in front of Beckett Walsh's door. The gold numbers glinted at her, as if reveling in her forthcoming mortification.

Hovering, McKenna pulled her compact out of her bag to check her makeup. If she was going to throw her dignity to the wolves, she may as well look good while doing it. The plum and black eye makeup she'd worn to work had the right amount of don't-fuck-with-me vibes. Plus, she'd swapped out her matte nude lipstick for a more exciting wet-shine gloss at the counter today, which made her look even more fierce. She might get out of this unscathed.

Key word: might.

. . .

I cannot, in good conscience, invest in the very thing that has caused my daughter so much pain. You no longer have my support, financial or otherwise.

The words replayed in Beckett Walsh's head, hot bubbling rage burning a path up the back of his throat. Lionus Aldridge knew he was killing Beckett's dream and everything he'd been working toward. This app was going to provide a secure and comfortable future for his mother, allowing Beckett to *finally* help her out of her "living week to week" cycle for good. It would cement him as a force within the technology industry and give his company, M.K. Technologies, the prestige it needed to play in the big leagues. He'd be safe. Stable. And so would his family.

Not to mention the fact that his idea was solid. No, scratch that.

It was brilliant.

WealthHack was a virtual financial adviser—relying on the voice command technology that already existed for so much more than simply sending texts and emails. The idea was to sync the app to your online banking and investment accounts so that your WealthHack assistant could provide daily, weekly, or monthly reports on spending habits. It could also be set up to provide alerts if spending categories went over the budgeted amount—i.e., if you'd spent too much on entertainment activities one week—and provided daily reminders of your wealth-management goals. For people who were trying to improve their spending habits, the app would also give tips on where more economical choices could be made by scanning the cost of items across major online retailers.

The plan was to start the app within Australia only, since it would be important to get representatives from the four major banks on board. By not jumping straight into an international release, Beckett would be able to get the product to beta testing more quickly, and then he could expand the app beyond that. The initial goal was to have WealthHack go Australia-wide, with an option on a smaller New Zealand release. But Beckett was convinced this had worldwide potential…and Lionus had thought so, too, at the beginning. The guy was a businessman at heart, so Sherri must have said something particularly heinous to get him to back down.

Two million dollars. Poof! Gone. Money that would pay the app developers he'd hired, his marketing activities, the office space he'd found. Money that would cover his living costs while he devoted every waking second to this one idea. His *golden* idea. All his eggs were in one basket and his fiancée—*ex*-fiancée—had taken a hammer to the lot.

Which was why he'd been at JGL Investments today. Looking for a venture capitalist at this super early stage wasn't ideal. He didn't have enough together to ask for seed funding, which meant they would be looking for a bigger slice of the pie. More risk always meant a bigger cut.

And that left *him*, the creator, as a code minion. They'd asked for a sixty-forty split of the profit, feature approval, and naming rights.

Bloody naming rights!

There was no way he would be handing over that kind of power. What would be the point in getting investors in if they were going to take all his control away? He may as well re-enter the rat race and forget about the app all together.

Not. Going. To. Happen.

He needed to think of a solution for how to smooth things over with Sherri. It was the only way forward he could see. Sure, it sounded a little callous, but he simply wanted everything to go back to normal. He wanted his relationship with his fiancée, his startup, and his life to be smooth sailing.

Regret squeezed around his heart like a fist. His relationship with Sherri hadn't been a bed of roses, but they were compatible. Companionable. They had a shared interest in business and making a solid foundation for their future. All the things he knew made for a good match. They should have worked.

Should have, but didn't.

Unfortunately, the demise of his relationship with Sherri wasn't only a personal blow. It was now a business one, too.

"This is a temporary setback," he said, taking a deep breath. "You *will* find a way to fix this."

He had too much riding on their relationship to let it go without a fight. For the time being he'd give Sherri space to cool down, and that would give him time to come up with a plan.

Taking another deep breath, Beckett eyed the box sitting on his dining table, trying to remember what he'd ordered. He was waiting on a new computer case, but that wasn't supposed to come until Wednesday. Perhaps they'd shipped it express. Having something to tinker with would help keep his mind busy.

Since his plans were balancing on a knife's edge, it would do him some good to unwind for an hour before he jumped back into work mode. He sliced along the tape keeping the box closed.

He reached into the box and pulled out what appeared to be a surprisingly lifelike vibrator. "What the hell?"

This wasn't exactly the kind of distraction he had in mind.

An invoice was neatly tucked in between the boxes of the sex toys. Yep, it was his address all right, but the name at the top was Noelle Smith. He knew for a fact that there was no one on this floor named Noelle. Not that he knew everyone personally, but he had a memory like a steel trap. Not quite eidetic, but close enough. It served him well in business, being able to recall names and the content of emails and contracts with ease. Which made up for the fact that he was often a little rough around the edges in the area of building relationships.

Nope, there was definitely not a Noelle on level one. They had a Norah in 106—a chef, Sherri had told him once— and a Nathan in 109. But he wasn't sure what Nathan or his boyfriend would want with something called a Satisfier Pro Clitoral Stimulator.

What about it made it pro, exactly?

He placed the invoice back on top of the box and sighed. How was he supposed to explain to the concierge that he'd opened it? Wasn't it a crime to open someone else's mail? He should've taken a second to look at the name on the box before he sliced into it. But he'd been desperate for something to distract him from the shock of Sherri's news and Lionus's email.

A knock sounded at the door. Three short raps, succinct. Hesitant, maybe. Not Sherri, since she still had a key. And not his sister, Kayla, who always knocked a tune that she would then make him guess. He'd only ever gotten it right once. "Eye of the Tiger" was hard to mistake.

Beckett checked the peephole and saw the top of a dark head. He flicked the lock and pulled the door open, his breath catching in his throat when he saw who it was.

McKenna Prescott. Apartment 101. She worked at a cosmetics counter in the Wentworth Department store on Bourke Street. He knew that because she'd given Sherri a few samples one time.

McKenna must have come straight from work—a badge that said "CAM-Ready Cosmetics, McKenna" was pinned at her right breast. And she wore that dark smudgy stuff around her eyes that always made his blood surge a little faster through his veins. She looked sultry. When her tongue darted out to run along the bottom of one very shiny, very plump bottom lip, he swallowed hard.

The woman was a late-night fantasy personified. Which was precisely why he avoided her at all costs, especially when she tried to talk to him in the mailroom.

"Hi," she said, with an expression that was almost a smile…but not quite. Her hands toyed nervously with the ends of her hair, which were dyed a bright Barney the dinosaur purple. The shade was in striking contrast with her blue eyes. The whole effect was…stimulating.

"Can I help you?" he asked.

"I'm sorry to bother you, but I'm…uhhh." She cringed, her eyes darting down the hallway as if planning an escape route. "I think you may have something of mine."

He raised a brow. Not likely. The one time he'd ended up with something of hers—a notice about an apartment inspection that had accidentally been stuck to a letter from his bank—he'd slipped it into her mailbox. The thought of hand delivering it had streaked across his mind, but he shut it down quickly. McKenna had a strange effect on him, and not one that he wanted to explore.

You could explore it now. It's over with Sherri, so what's the harm?

No. He wanted his fiancée back and he wasn't going to mess up his chances by indulging in a silly fantasy.

"I, um…" She tugged on her hair again. "I had a parcel delivered and I think you ended up with it. I typed my address too quickly and got the numbers mixed up. If I could just have it back—"

"Noelle Smith?" His brain whirred and Beckett could swear he heard a sizzling sound as if someone had poured Coke over a hot motherboard.

Good Lord, he did not need to picture McKenna and the Satisfier Pro Clitoral Stimulator.

"It's my alias for when I don't want to use my real name." She let out a nervous laugh. "Don't ask why."

He didn't need to, he *knew*. But now how the hell was he supposed to explain that he'd opened what was obviously a very private purchase? Could he claim that he'd never received the parcel and then leave it by her door in the dead of night?

"The concierge told me you picked it up," she said. Her teeth dented her lower lip. "By mistake, of course."

Fuck. "I did."

The excruciating silence stretched on while she looked up at him with those big blue eyes, imploring him not to make her ask for it. But he was tongue-tied. His mind stuck on the image of her using the toys on herself. His imagination had sketched out in vivid detail how her gorgeous face would look, eyes screwed shut and her glossy lips parted, as she slipped a hand down her body…

"Can I grab it?" she asked.

Hell yes, you can grab it.

"Excuse me?" He blinked.

"My parcel." She raised a brow. "Can I grab it?"

"Uh, sure." He stepped aside and held the door open for her, since it was the last possible gentlemanly thing he could do. Not only had he invaded her privacy, but he'd mentally undressed her while doing it.

Good work, Beckett. That's some A-Grade assholery right there.

"It's through here." He held the door for her and shut it with a soft *click*. The sound fired through his body like a gunshot. "I…it's open."

"What?" Her head snapped up to his, her cheeks burning bright red while the rest of her complexion was drained of its natural hue. "You opened my mail?"

He cursed himself internally. "I was distracted and didn't check the name."

"Did you see what was inside?" Her faced begged him to lie, but Beckett was—for better or worse—honest about everything. He cleared his throat. "Just what was on top... and the invoice."

Good lord. If he'd only seen the toys, that would be one thing. Seen, reacted, and let his imagination run riot was a *whole* other level of trouble.

Chapter Two

"Oh God." McKenna dropped her head into her hands. "Can this day get any worse?"

Which items had he seen? The clip-on vibrating butterfly? The strawberry-scented lube? Mr. Whopper?

She forced herself to lower her hands and make eye contact. Now was not the time to regress to toddler-style denial, no matter how much she wanted to crawl into a hole and never come out. Did he have to be *so* good looking? That was making it so much harder.

Beckett towered over her—though at five foot four it wasn't uncommon to have to look up at people—and he was built like an athlete. Strong and solid, lean like an AFL player but with a broad chest that filled out his blue shirt perfectly. He had wavy dark blond hair that was cut short and neat, the hint of stubble barely breaking through along his jaw.

So conservative, so not her type at *all*. He looked like someone her mother would have picked out, and yet her body never failed to sing when he was around. And no church hymns, either. Oh no. Right now they were singing some

Marvin Gaye-level shit.

"I'm not judging you," he said. His expression was difficult to read, but it didn't sound like he was lying. Though there was definitely something strange in the air. Tension, maybe.

Just your ability to embarrass yourself sucking the life out of the room.

"You can, it's a pretty ridiculous scenario." Her gaze darted to where her package sat on his dining table. The corner of a pink box poked out of the top, the word "cum" making her cringe. "Have a laugh when your girlfriend gets home. I promise, I won't be offended."

"That won't happen." He shook his head, a crease forming between his brows.

McKenna snorted. "You're a better person than me, then."

"I mean, she won't be coming home."

"Oh." She wasn't sure what else to say, but Beckett was staring at her as though he expected something. A reaction, or maybe some solidarity. "Uh, is it permanent?"

He shook his head, looking every bit the picture of male bewilderment. "Who the hell knows?"

She'd met the woman a few times. Shirley…or something like that. Her name had reminded McKenna of old fifties screwball comedies, and it'd seemed at odds with the woman's careful, slightly uptight persona. She'd visited the CAM-Ready cosmetics counter once, looking for a new lipstick that was "out of her comfort zone." McKenna had suggested a vibrant poppy red, but the woman had ended up going for a pink-toned nude instead of her usual beige-toned nude.

"If it makes you feel any better, I got dumped, too." She jerked her head toward the box. "Hence the toys."

Beckett's brows creased and it looked like he was about to lecture her, though for what she had no idea. God, how did the man manage to look sexier than sin while wearing an expression better suited to an angry school principal?

Clearly Gage screwed with your head so much you no longer know what or who you're attracted to. Maybe you should have ordered a sex doll as well. Tap out of personal interaction altogether.

"Why were you dumped?" he asked.

McKenna blinked. She hadn't thought this situation could get any stranger, but here they were talking about their love lives while ignoring the box of shame, as she'd come to think of it. Beckett had never said much of anything to her, let alone asked her a personal question. She wasn't sure what to make of it.

"He wanted to get serious…just not with me. I'm not wife material, it would seem."

Beckett bobbed his head. "I understand."

"You're not supposed to agree with him." She folded her arms across her chest, indignation burning holes in her cheeks. "That's rude."

"I didn't say I agreed, I said I understood," he replied, his voice tinted with irritation. There was that school principal look again.

"Close enough," she huffed.

"No, it's not. Agreeing and understanding are two totally different things." He threw his hands up in the air. "I don't get why women insist on twisting words so they can be insulted about something that isn't meant to be an insult. It's so… confusing."

Wow. A sentence with more than five words? Obviously she'd hit a hot button. It seemed as though her initial summations about him had been spot on—smokin' hot but slightly awkward. Maybe not the best with people. An introvert. Temptation needled at her; she wanted to keep Beckett talking. She wanted to find out more about him.

"So you said something to piss your girlfriend off, huh? That why she dumped you?"

"You're assuming I know why she dumped me," he drawled.

Had Beckett Walsh given her...sass? For some reason this pleased her greatly. There *was* more to him than robotic greetings and a master's degree in avoiding human contact.

"How can you not know?" She laughed. "Usually getting dumped is the point where the other person lists all your flaws."

He looked at her more closely. "You sound experienced in getting dumped."

That. Smug. Bastard.

"Excuse me, Mr. Attitude. Maybe it's that I simply know what's going on around me, because I'm not stuck in my own world all the time like *some* people." Pause. "And by some people, I mean you, if there was any uncertainty."

"I'm not in my own world." He didn't sound convinced.

"Tell me," she said, leaning on one hip and cocking her head. "Why did you say you understood why my boyfriend broke up with me?"

A fleeting expression rippled across his face—something that looked like the lovechild of wariness and irritation. "Why do you want to know?"

"Call it curiosity."

His eyes raked her up and down, the quick and assessing gaze should have felt analytical. Distant. But instead it felt as though she'd lowered herself into a warm bath, and her body was melting into the heat.

"I understand that for some men you might be too... sparkly."

Okay, so that wasn't what she was expecting. "Too sparkly?"

His Adam's apple bobbed. "Yes. You stand out."

"Does that mean you've noticed me around?" She tried not to sound gleeful, but for some reason the thought was very gratifying.

Remember that thing about not getting involved with men for a while? Besides, you don't want to be rebound fodder.

"I know who you are." He nodded, but he gave nothing away.

McKenna had the feeling that was Beckett's MO. But tonight she'd obviously caught him in a rare vulnerable moment where he'd been rattled enough to talk to her. It would have been easy enough for him to hand over the box of shame and send her packing.

But he didn't.

"You're usually a man of few words, aren't you?" she said.

"That's what my sister tells me."

"I didn't know you had a sister." Really, she didn't know anything about him. Other than the fact that he had this hot, nerdy vibe going on and it was eliciting some very strange reactions in her.

"Her name is Kayla," he said. "You'd like her. She talks a lot, too."

"I'm going to assume you don't mean that as an insult."

"I don't."

"What does she do? Is she married? Do you have adorable nieces and nephews?" The questions tumbled out of her lips. When people were locked up tight with personal information, it only made her more curious. And, despite knowing she should grab her box and move on, McKenna couldn't help herself.

"She's in PR. Engaged. No kids."

Short. Succinct. So Beckett.

McKenna prided herself on being able to read people—it was a key component of her job. When someone sat down in her makeup chair, she had to read between the lines about what they wanted—feel around for the edge of their comfort zone, so she could wow them without overwhelming them. To be able to make an impact on how someone viewed themselves, she had to first figure out who they were.

And Lordy, did she ever want to dig around in Beckett's mind right now. But that wasn't a good idea for either of them. And he had a point, she *was* an expert in being dumped...or rather, picking the wrong men. Which meant it was time to put an end to this strange little conversation and quash any ideas that she should ask Beckett to have a drink with her.

"I should get going," she said, walking past him and picking up her box. She tried not to cringe at the hot-pink clit stimulator staring up at her. "Thanks for...uh, babysitting my parcel."

He made a noise that was probably intended to sound like "you're welcome" but without using any actual words. Tempting as it was to tease him, she really needed to get the hell out before she made any more bad decisions. Beckett stood like a sexy man-mountain and watched her intently as she shifted from foot to foot, her lady parts battling with her brain.

While his neat blue shirt and chinos gave off a conservative Clark Kent kind of vibe, his eyes were something else completely. Something unwieldly and heart-stoppingly masculine. Something that caused sensation to ripple through her, snapping its teeth at the small vestige of willpower she was trying to muster up.

He was so damn...unnerving.

"I guess I'll see you around," she said, heading to the door.

His long legs got him there first and he opened it for her, that white-hot gaze still singeing her from the inside out. He didn't smile, but at least now he was making eye contact. Progress.

What progress? You don't want any goddamn progress!

And she'd repeat it a thousand times a day if it meant that she'd be able to stick to her guns.

McKenna let her front door shut behind her, and then she sagged against it, the box of sex toys heavy in her hands. For some unknown reason, her heart was tripping on itself. The *ba-dum, ba-dum* rhythm making her all jittery and fizzy, like her veins had been filled with champagne instead of blood.

Beckett freaking Walsh. The guy was so not her speed—too introverted, too much the strong, silent type. Like one of those old school cowboys who didn't say much but could somehow make you swoon with a mere raise of his brow.

She wondered if he had Facebook. McKenna stifled a giggle by sinking her teeth into her bottom lip. Just because she'd made the right decision not to invite Beckett over didn't mean she was above a little masochistic internet stalking.

She dumped the box on her kitchen table and headed to her couch, grabbing her laptop on the way. Beckett didn't seem like the kind of guy who would be into social media, but she might luck out and find an abandoned Facebook profile. Or maybe something on LinkedIn.

Her nails clicked over the keys. There were a bunch of articles about a computer program that Beckett had sold—something to do with time recording for employers. Not exactly juicy reading. She was out of luck with Facebook and Twitter...but then she stumbled across a picture of Beckett and his ex from some charity event. The caption under the photo said Beckett Walsh and Sherri Aldridge. McKenna snapped her fingers. *That's* what her name was.

They looked good together in that cardboard cutout way—matching gold hair and serious expressions. There didn't appear to be an ounce of love in their eyes. But perhaps they'd been taken by surprise. The photo didn't look posed.

Sherri, on the other hand, *was* on Facebook. Her status was single, and there weren't too many photos available. One, however, was tagged with a woman named Kayla Walsh. Beckett's younger sister. The resemblance was subtle—her hair was more light brown than his blond, her complexion a little more olive-toned. But they both had vibrant eyes in the exact same shade of aquamarine.

McKenna clicked onto Kayla's profile and gasped. A post announcing her upcoming wedding sat at the top, which shouldn't have been surprising given Beckett had told her as much not ten minutes ago. But it wasn't the fact that she was getting married that captured McKenna's attention...it was the identity of the groom-to-be.

Aaron Michael Corbett Jr.

The guy could only have sounded more important if they'd tacked "esquire" onto the end of his name. The Corbett family were a big deal. Their company was into a lot of things—freight, transportation, logistics, storage. And they were frequently in the media, which was why McKenna knew about them.

So Beckett's little sister was getting married to the grandson of one of Melbourne's most influential men. Her heartbeat picked up, excitement bubbling in her chest. This was *exactly* the kind of wedding McKenna needed to give her freelance business the boost it desperately needed. Her big break.

A wedding like this would mean pictures of her work in the society pages and on wedding blogs. It would mean increased word-of-mouth referrals. It might just give her enough clients to quit CAM-Ready Cosmetics.

McKenna grinned. Fate had brought her to Beckett Walsh's doorstep. Now all she needed to do was convince

Beckett to put her forward for the job.

• • •

The following afternoon, McKenna bounced up and down on the soles of her hot-pink Converse sneakers outside Beckett's door. Funny how she was here again, and not any less nervous than yesterday. Asking for help never came easy to her, no doubt a product of her upbringing. The Prescott family made Type-A people look like free-spirited hippies. Success and prestige were the names of the game and asking for help was frowned upon. McKenna had learned from a young age that she was destined to disappoint. In her mind, it was easier to fail quietly than misguidedly attempt success and then draw everyone's attention for the inevitable.

But today she was taking destiny into her own hands.

Sucking in a breath, she raised her fist and let it fall just under the gleaming 110 on Beckett's door. There were no sounds from the inside. Maybe he wasn't home? Or maybe he'd looked through the peephole and decided he couldn't deal with her today.

McKenna leaned forward, pressing her ear to the door. Only silence greeted her, but then the door moved and she stumbled, her hand reaching out for something to grab onto. Her fingers met hard muscle, bare skin. Water.

"What the hell?" Beckett's hands shot out to steady her, but not before she'd slipped and brushed the towel knotted at his waist. Not before she'd brushed the solid bulge beneath it. "McKenna?"

"Beckett!" His name sounded like a squeak, high-pitched enough to have all the dogs in South Melbourne running. "I'm sorry. I didn't mean to…"

Oh God. How did one finish that sentence?

I'm sorry I was listening in to your apartment? I'm sorry

I accidentally touched your cock? I'm sorry I'm kind of tempted to do it again?

He checked to make sure that she wasn't going to fall before he released her. "You didn't mean to…?"

"Interrupt." Her gaze ran over his naked torso and the wet mop of dark blond hair on his head. His chest was covered in delicious blond fuzz. "You were obviously in the shower."

"Obviously." The corner of his lips twitched.

Was he annoyed or amused? She never could tell. One thing she *could* tell, however, was that Beckett was breaking every damn computer nerd stereotype there was. No way he was living on Burger Rings and Mountain Dew with that body. He wasn't bulky like a gym junkie, rather he looked lean. Hard.

Tom Hiddletson with an Australian accent.

"Can I help you with something?" He raised a brow. "You did knock, didn't you?"

"I did." McKenna's voice sounded weird to her own ears, probably because her body was too busy firing up her hormonal system rather than remembering to do the important things…like breathing. "I need a favor."

"I don't usually get asked for favors while I'm wearing a towel." There was that twitch again.

"Did you just make a joke?"

"I guess if you have to ask, then probably not." He motioned for her to sit on his couch. "Give me minute."

"Sure, of course. Take your time, there's no rush at all."

A simple "okay" would have sufficed.

Against her better judgment, McKenna watched Beckett as he walked away, her gaze transfixed on his tight butt moving beneath the fluffy white towel. Holy crap, did she want to follow him into his bedroom and rip that annoying piece of fabric from his body.

Just freaking great. Three days into this whole no-men

thing and she was already climbing the walls. Mr. Whopper was no replacement for the real thing, it seemed.

"What happened to Operation Self-Love?" she muttered to herself. "You're here for your career. Now suck it up."

She tugged on the hem of her long-sleeved T-shirt—which was an old CAM-Ready promo top with a pair of big pink lips on the front—and steeled herself. All she had to do was ask for his help. Simple.

And maybe convince him it wasn't super creepy that she'd been looking him up online. Unfortunately, she didn't seem to have a single friend in common with either Beckett's sister or his ex, so she couldn't use that...or could she? Beckett himself didn't have Facebook. It might be easy enough to fabricate a distant connection.

No, she wasn't going to lie. McKenna Prescott might not be the shining academic star her parents dreamed of, but she wasn't a liar.

Beckett returned to the lounge room wearing a pair of jeans and a soft T-shirt that looked sexy and snuggly. It was fitted across his shoulders and chest, rocketing the memory of touching him to the front of her mind. He dropped down into the chair across from her, bracing his forearms against his thighs. It was incredible how he could command her complete attention without saying a word.

"Thanks for letting me in...again," she said after the silence stretched on a heartbeat longer than was comfortable. "I don't want to take up too much of your time."

He motioned for her to continue, using a subtle rotation of his wrist. Her gaze was drawn to how the muscle and skin moved with the joint, to the smattering of blond hair that covered his arm. To all the finer details she'd overlooked on pretty much everyone else. But he was the kind of guy who made you want to revel in the details.

"So, when we were chatting yesterday you mentioned

that your sister is engaged. I'm trying to launch my freelance makeup business and I'm looking for clients, especially ones like your sister who are going to have big weddings." She sucked in a breath. "It would mean the world to me if you'd put my name forward."

Beckett's brows wrinkled. "How do you know she's having a big wedding?"

Of course he didn't miss a beat. "I was looking you up online and I saw who she's engaged to."

McKenna sucked in a breath and mentally crossed her fingers. An excited flip deep in her gut told her that this was the opportunity she'd been waiting for. And the feeling had absolutely *nothing* to do with the sexy man in front of her.

Chapter Three

Beckett wasn't sure how to react. Had she looked him up because she wanted to know about him…or because she'd seen the opportunity for her business? He couldn't really be annoyed if that was the case. After all, he knew what it took to start a business from scratch. McKenna was certainly ballsy, something that would serve her well. But there was a tiny, egotistical part of him that hoped she'd been trying to find out more about *him*.

Why? So you can be further tempted by something that's off-limits? You know this can't go anywhere.

"It sounds a lot creepier than it really is." A nervous smile flittered across her pink lips. "I promise."

Her lipstick was the exact same bubblegum shade as her sneakers and the design on her top. So perfectly matched, he would have bet money that they had the same RGB code. He wondered briefly if the inside of her apartment was similarly vibrant, in contrast to the stark minimalist white he'd picked for his place.

"Are you annoyed?" She cocked her head, her blue eyes

inspecting him. "I can't tell. You don't say much. Well, you said a little yesterday, of course. But I mean usually. When I say hi you tend to just…grunt."

"No I don't."

Her button nose wrinkled. "So you can't say hello back but you can argue with me about the sound you make?"

"Yes."

Her nostrils flared and damn if it wasn't the most adorable thing ever. "Why don't you ever say hello to me?"

All his life people had asked him why he was so quiet. Some assumed he was hiding a secret, other guessed it was a negotiation tactic. An old friend had once teased him that it was all a ruse to make him appear mysterious. But the truth was, he only said what was necessary. What was the point of contributing to all the useless, brainless chatter that filled people's heads? The world had gotten so…noisy.

He leaned back in his chair. "Are you here to ask for my help or to question my communication abilities?"

"Can't I do both?" Her lips tugged up into a smile. It was like being blinded by the midday sun.

Helping McKenna wasn't a smart idea. He could already see how it would go—McKenna and Kayla would become instant friends, and then she'd be further inserted into his life via family events. Not to mention the wedding itself. Kayla would be *certain* that McKenna would make a better girlfriend than Sherri, and would do her best to set him up. It'd happened before.

"I wish I could help you, but I can't. My sister's wedding is her business and I don't want to get involved." *That* wasn't a lie.

"All you have to do is pass on my business card," she said, her eyes pleading with him. They were framed by impossibly long eyelashes that made her look Bambi-like. "Tell her I'm your super nice lady friend from down the hall and that I'm very good at my job."

"You're not my lady friend." Beckett recoiled at the uneven thump in his chest. "I barely know you. How can I recommend you?"

He'd been asked to put his name to other people's talents in the past. But he had a strict rule when it came to business— never say anything you can't stake your reputation on.

"How can you say you don't know me? You've been grunting at my hellos for over a year now." Her expression told him that she would not be deterred. "Or get your ex to vouch for me, then. She's visited me a few times at the makeup counter."

"Pushy, aren't you?"

"It's one of my better qualities." Her eyes sparkled mischievously. "My big brother told me once that I was scrappy, but I think I prefer pushy."

"I don't doubt your abilities." He raked a hand through his hair, feeling like a bastard. But she'd wedged herself into his brain. He couldn't have it. "Kayla is adamant about doing the wedding *her* way. She wants to be free to make her own decisions."

"I'm asking for an introduction, that's all. Please." She knotted her hands in her lap and leaned forward. "If there's anything I can do to even the score, I'll do it."

This was *not* helping the situation. The way she looked at him—that beautiful face beaming with sincerity—while she promised to even the score, was making him think a whole lot of things he shouldn't. Dirty things. The kind of things that made him hot and horny and more than a little bit uncomfortable.

She threw her hands up in the air. "Hell, if I can help you get your girlfriend back I'll even do that."

"You can't do that." His brain tried to process the offer. "Can you?"

"Sure. I'm an expert matchmaker." Something strange flickered in the depths of her eyes. "That is, assuming you want her back."

"I do." The words came immediately, though it left him with a hardness in his chest. A tension that hadn't been there a moment ago.

Of course he wanted Sherri back. Isn't that exactly what he'd been trying to do ever since she stormed out of his apartment?

"How about we trade? You give me a recommendation, and I'll do my best to help you win back the girl of your dreams." She picked at a hole in her jeans where part of her thigh was exposed. "I can't guarantee anything, but then neither can you."

He thought about it. Having a woman's input might help him fix this situation. But, more importantly, it might help him fix the situation *quickly.* He was confident that things would work themselves out as they always did, but now he was under a deadline. One month until the money ran out.

But that would mean spending more time with McKenna…

However, if she was supposed to be the one helping him get Sherri back then that should throttle the possibility of anything happening between them. She would know he wanted another woman, and he would be able to keep his eye on what mattered.

"Matchmaking isn't the same as fixing a relationship," he said eventually.

McKenna had managed to keep quiet while he'd been processing this information, but her fidgeting had steadily increased until she was tapping her nails against the edge of his couch. "Sure it is. It's all about making two people see that they're perfect for one another."

"And how do you do that?"

She sat up straighter, drawing her shoulders back as she smiled at him with confidence. "I learn what makes them tick up there." She nodded to his head. "In there"—her gaze dropped to his chest—"and down there." Her eyes lingered for a second in his lap, before her cheeks flushed. It was so wrong for his pulse to spike and all the blood in his body to change direction and head south, while he was planning to get his ex back. So fucking wrong.

She's an attractive woman and you're a red-blooded man, it's natural. But the difference between you and an animal is that you can hide those feelings away and not do anything about it. You can control it.

It was true. Feelings meant nothing if you didn't act on them. And if there was one thing Beckett had been doing his whole life, it was thinking with his head, rather than his heart.

"Okay," he said, standing and extending his hand. "You've got yourself a deal."

• • •

Later that night, McKenna sat on her couch leafing through takeaway menus, having no idea what she felt like. Thai food? The delivery guy had made a crack about how she was their most loyal customer, so maybe it was time to lay off the pad thai and satay sticks. Pizza? Too greasy. Indian food? Eh, she didn't feel like anything spicy.

A knock at the door made her spring off the couch. For some reason her mind immediately drifted to Beckett, which was stupid. They'd agreed to check in after he'd spoken to his sister about her wedding. So why would he be here?

No real reason, just the stupid fantasies that you've been making up in your head.

"Remember how you agreed to help him get his fiancée

back?" she grumbled to herself as she wrapped her hand around the doorknob.

That meant no more dirty thoughts. And no more fantasies about him turning up here, unannounced.

McKenna pulled the door open to find her best friend Emery standing there. She raised a brow and pushed her chunky black glasses farther up her nose. "Do you usually answer the door sans pants?"

McKenna looked down at her bare legs, extending out from the bottom of her boy short undies. "Count yourself lucky I wore a T-shirt."

Truth was, pants had been the last thing on her mind after her visit to Beckett. Which was a problem.

"What happened?" Emery's gaze slipped over the mess in McKenna's apartment as she walked in, letting the door swing shut behind her.

"Oh yeah, that."

The night McKenna had decided to get drunk and order a box of sex toys—the night that had set all the wheels in motion for Operation Self-Love—had started with her getting dumped. Publicly.

Her "date night" outfit of a glittery miniskirt, slinky blue tank top, and chunky cork wedges still lay in a heap on the floor, from when she'd stormed into her apartment, stomping around like a baby elephant throwing a tantrum.

Emery wrinkled her nose. "I would ask if you've got someone hidden away, but I doubt you'd invite me in if that was the case."

McKenna sighed. "Gage dumped me. And I've been wallowing, instead of cleaning my apartment."

"I told you not to trust a guy who sounds like he was named after a *Bold and the Beautiful* character." Emery sighed and patted her arm. "Can I just say 'insert comforting statement here' and be done with it?"

"You're all heart, Em." McKenna rolled her eyes and dropped the menus onto her coffee table with a slap.

"What did he say?"

"That he got a promotion at work and now he needs to start taking his life seriously. That I'm a lot of 'fun,' but he wants to stop screwing around." She made a gagging noise in the back of her throat. "Apparently, girls who like glitter aren't serious. He needs someone who 'gives back' to the community and does work that makes society a better place."

That was the bit that stung most. Because her parents had said things with a similar sentiment over the years. Why didn't she want to get a "real" job and help people like her doctor brothers?

Your work makes a difference, too. There's nothing *wrong with helping women find confidence through makeup.*

She knew that, of course. Nothing would sway her from the belief that makeup was a form of creative expression. The moment she held a mirror up to her client's face and saw their joy, it was the most empowering feeling in the world.

"Did you tell him to shove his judgmental comments where the sun doesn't shine?"

"Better. I told him that I'm glad we were breaking up because I was starting to get so used to faking orgasms that I was worried I'd forget what the real thing felt like."

"You didn't." Emery threw her head back and laughed. "I wish I was there."

"The response was underwhelming. He didn't care." McKenna sighed. "So you'll be happy to know I'm officially out of the dating game now. My crazy cat lady starter kit is on the way and I've bought enough sex toys to make a cam girl jealous."

Emery dropped down onto the couch. "Good for you. It's about time you came to the dark side."

"Aren't you going to give me any sympathy at all?"

McKenna rolled her eyes. Sometimes Emery took her "man repeller" status a little too seriously.

"Look." Emery patted the empty spot next to her on the couch. "You know I'm not a touchy-feely kinda gal. How about I take you out and ply you with drinks, instead?"

"I don't want to go out," she grumbled as she dropped down next to her friend. "I want to stay home and consume my body weight in ice cream like you're supposed to during a breakup."

The funny thing was, however, she didn't actually feel that bad. Maybe knowing that she had a plan in place was enough to keep her spirits buoyed. This time she was going to take charge of her life and find the success she craved, rather than pinning all her hopes on some man.

Probably a good idea since your ability to choose the right men leaves a lot to be desired.

"Don't look at it as a breakup, Mac. He's unlocked your shackles." Emery slid a comforting arm around her shoulders. "Trust me, this is a good thing. You weren't happy with him, anyway."

"I know." She nodded. "But I didn't want to be the dumpee for once."

"Okay, that's it." Emery pushed up and dragged McKenna with her. "This pity party is over right now. We're going out."

"No," McKenna whined. "I'm all prepared to wallow. Can't we just order in and watch *Game of Thrones*?"

Emery raised a brow. "That's really what you want?"

"It is. I'll even put pants on."

"Fine. You go get changed, I'll order." She leafed through the menus. "I vote Chinese food."

"Done." McKenna threw her arms around Emery and planted a kiss on her cheek.

She collected her clothing from the floor and headed into her bedroom. Her purse was still sitting where she'd thrown it on the bed earlier that day, the contents spilling out—her phone, keys, compact mirror, lipstick, lip gloss, and a tampon. The little blue light on her phone flashed, alerting her to a new text message.

Gage wanting to know if she was okay. Gage, again, hoping that he hadn't broken her heart too badly. Douche.

"Fuck you, Gage," she muttered at the phone, resisting the urge to hurl the device out of her window.

Emery was right, she hadn't been happy with him. He was far too uptight for her, far too worried about what other people thought. But he was the first guy who'd made a good impression on her impossible-to-please parents. And for once, she hadn't been made to feel like a bloody disappointment. Dr. Amy Prescott and Bert Prescott of Peterson, Prescott & Partners were not the type of parents to give her a pat on the head for the sake of it.

Stupid. You should have listened to your gut.

Instead of worrying about the sad state of her romantic opportunities, she was going to throw everything into advancing her career. By the end of the year she *would* be a freelance makeup artist, come hell or high water. All she needed was the right opportunity, and Beckett's sister's society wedding was it. Then she could leave her department store job behind and prove to herself that she *did* have the stuff to make it on her own.

She reached for a pair of leggings and tugged them up over her legs. Then she got to work on removing the pins from the elaborate updo holding her brown and purple hair hostage. The bobby pins hit her vanity with metallic clinks as she yanked them out one by one.

The people in her life might not understand her need to be bold and creative, but she was *done* trying to squish herself into some damn box. She was done worrying what other thought of her style and career choices.

Screw the naysayers, McKenna Prescott was going to be even brighter and more sparkly than ever.

"How's work?" Emery asked, when McKenna wandered back into the living room. "Have they promoted you to counter manager yet?"

"No." McKenna slumped back in her seat. "But I want out of retail, anyway. The sales aspect is exhausting and it's all KPIs and units per sale and daily targets and...ugh. I had a meeting with the area manager last week and she gave me hell over the fact that my average sale is seventy-six dollars instead of seventy-nine. Apparently, I'm pulling down the whole counter with numbers like that. I mean, seriously?"

"But you're great at sales." Emery cocked her head. "The girls I sent in to see you said they were only looking for a lipstick and they both ended buying a bunch of things."

"I spend too long with the customers, according to them. She said I talk to them too much and I should be cashing them out quicker so I can move on to the next customer." She huffed. "Never mind the fact that I have a bunch of customers who will *only* come to me because they know I don't treat them like numbers and just push whatever the company wants. They want us to act like call center staff."

"That's bullshit." Emery rolled her eyes.

"It is. I'm over it." She sighed. "I want to focus on the makeup application bit, that's what really inspires me. Not this sales crap."

"So you're really going to make the leap to freelancing?"

"Yeah, I am. But I'm not keen to make a leap into not being able to pay my rent. Freelance is competitive and we're not supposed to take appointments away from the counter, since that's how they guarantee people buy more products."

"Ah, so they won't let you hand out business cards, then?"

"No. I slip a few out here and there, but if the boss catches me I'll have my head on the chopping block. They

caught another girl and cut her hours down until she left."
She sighed. "I suspect it's coming more from the department
store than CAM-Ready, because they figure once people
get through the front door then they're likely to spend in
other departments, too. Which means it's tough to build up a
business outside work. But I've got something on the hook."

She thought about telling Emery the whole story with the
parcel delivery, but decided against it. No way in hell would
Emery *ever* let her live it down.

Besides, she'd learned a long time ago not to tell people
about her plans until she had a win to share. Too many times
she'd gotten excited and blurted out an opportunity, only to
have it crumble around her. Then she'd be putting herself in
the firing line, especially where her parents were concerned.

*See, McKenna, you should have stayed in university and
finished your law degree like we told you. Then you wouldn't
be struggling to get ahead.*

Nope. Not going down that path. Emery wasn't as bad as
her parents, but she certainly told it how it was and sometimes
McKenna needed a little more handholding than that.

A big part of Operation Self-Love was putting herself
first. And that meant keeping her big mouth shut until she
had something concrete to share.

Chapter Four

Beckett stared at his computer screen, willing inspiration to come. But ever since Lionus's email, the magic that had flowed from his fingertips a few days ago had dried up. He'd been staring at his laptop for hours and felt like he'd somehow gone backward instead of forward.

A buzzing sound cut into his thoughts and a picture of Kayla's face flashed on his phone's screen. It had been distorted with some kind of filter that made her look like a deer. Ridiculous. That was the last time he'd give his passcode to her.

"What have I said about changing the photos on my phone?"

"Well, hello to you, too, Mr. Grumpy-Pants." Kayla huffed on the other end of the line. "Which one did I use? Puppy face?"

"I think it's a deer...but you look stoned."

"Wow. Who pissed in your Wheaties this morning?"

"Sorry, Kay." He rubbed a hand up and down his face. "It's been a long week."

Beckett had made the decision not to tell Kayla about his current dilemma—she had her own things to worry about, like her wedding. And besides, Kayla was still holding out hope that he and Sherri would break up. For good. To say the two women in his life didn't get along would be an understatement. They both tried to be polite...emphasis on tried. It was all the more reason to keep the breakup a secret—she didn't need more ammunition should he and Sherri reconcile.

When you and Sherri reconcile.

"Good thing I called, then. I'm worried you'll forget how to speak if you don't have some human interaction." She laughed. "If you feel the urge to start communicating in binary, let me know. Okay?"

"Very funny." He rolled his eyes. "You'll be happy to know I had some human interaction last night."

"Ordering food from the Thai place doesn't count. You know that, right?" she teased.

"Actually, I had a chat with the girl who lives down the hall."

He wasn't about to mention that the only reason that happened was because she came to him. Irrelevant details... for the most part.

"A *cute* girl who lives down the hall?"

"She's an attractive woman," he said carefully.

Bloody hell. McKenna was an attractive woman in the same way that Elon Musk was a "smart" man. Technically correct, but wildly understated. Beckett wasn't the kind of guy to go ga-ga over a woman—never had, never would. He was far too logical for that. But still, McKenna's mere presence caused his brain to disconnect from his body. Every bloody time.

He didn't like it at all.

"There's a resounding compliment if I ever heard one,"

Kayla said with a snort.

"It *is* a compliment." He shrugged. "What else am I supposed to say. I'm in a relationship."

So then why had he been replaying their interactions over and over in his head? Why had he gone to bed thinking about how much he liked the way the stuff on her eyes glittered when she blinked. It made her look…magical.

"You can still notice the opposite sex," Kayla said.

He shook his head. Time for a change of topic. "How's Mum?"

Pause. "She's okay."

"Gee, don't go into such a detailed report, I haven't got all day," he said drily. The silence on the other end of the line had his intuition prickling. "What's going on?"

His sister sighed. "There was an incident at the supermarket."

Shit. His mother had worked as a supermarket cashier his whole life—but back then she also juggled it with a second job stacking shelves at the local Kmart. In the last few years, she'd been able to survive on one job, with help from Beckett. And she'd been at the same supermarket in that time, which was a relief. However, the business had been sold a few months back. His mother hadn't sounded too keen on her new boss last time he spoke to her.

"What incident?"

"How do I put this?" Kayla clucked her tongue. "She got into an altercation with the new manager over a change in the process for how they count the registers."

"And?"

"They fired her."

"What? They fired her for arguing about a process change?" He rubbed at his temple. "That's ridiculous."

"Well, technically they fired her for throwing a stapler." Kayla paused. "At her boss."

He groaned. "Why the hell would she do that?"

"You know what she's like, Becks. I love the woman, but when she gets a bee in her bonnet about something…"

His mother had a sense of righteousness that had caused her to lose jobs with frequency over their childhood. She had an issue with authority—something Beckett understood, since he vastly preferred working for himself over being a corporate drone. The difference was, however, that Beckett had sucked it up for years to support his family. He'd flipped burgers, taken shit from customers, and held his tongue all through high school and university so he could pay for his textbooks and contribute to the bills at home.

The security of his family was more important than his own desires. But his mother just couldn't keep her mouth shut sometimes. Throwing a stapler? Christ.

"She's lucky they didn't press charges," he said. "What's she doing now?"

"Cooling off. I told her to get her butt back in there tomorrow and throw herself on her sword." Kayla snorted. "But we both know what the chances of that happening are."

"Well, I made sure she has enough in the bank account to cover her rent for the duration of her lease. But she can use that for bills and I'll top it up once we start seeing some money come in from investors."

"You enable her, Becks."

"I take care of her, the way she took care of us for years," he said sharply.

Sure, his mother wasn't perfect. But she managed to raise two kids on her own—despite being a widow, then marrying a neglectful son of a bitch who never did anything to help her. All while encouraging her son and daughter to chase the best lives possible.

He and Kayla had received a decent education thanks to her pulling two jobs for decades. He couldn't say he was close to his mother, because he barely spent time with her growing up—but he knew how much she'd sacrificed to make sure they had clothes on their backs and food on their table. If her workplace temper was the worst thing he had to deal with, then he could manage it.

No way was he going to let her down.

"I could always ask Aaron—"

"No, this is *our* family. I'll take care of it."

He stared at his laptop screen again.

The numbers said Beckett's project could last six weeks without Lionus's investment. Four, if he wanted to continue eating and paying his bills. Thank God he'd bought his apartment after he'd sold his last computer system. At the time, his friends had given him hell—after all, weren't young, successful entrepreneurs supposed to splash their wealth around? Buy a sports car and some designer suits to lure the ladies in, they'd said.

Beckett had scoffed. Not his style. So he'd bought himself a modest one-bedroom apartment in a nice suburb that was close to the city, and paid for it in full. Then he'd researched cars and bought a low-level ex-lease Mercedes. It was enough to make him look successful when attending meetings without completely killing his savings. He'd put enough aside to cover his mother's rent for the next two years—with the promise that he'd secure her a permanent place once his next project paid dividends—and banked the remainder for a rainy day.

No lavish holidays, no shiny gadgets, and no personal indulgences. It was supposed to have been the perfect plan. Not having a mortgage hanging over his head was certainly helping him now, but the numbers didn't lie. With his mother losing her job, if he didn't fix this situation ASAP everything would come to a grinding halt. Beckett knew better than anyone that this kind of setback was enough to kill a startup dead in the water.

"Becks, you don't have to do everything by yourself," Kayla said quietly. "You know once I'm married, I'll pay you back everything I owe you for my degree."

"That was a gift, Kay. Not a loan."

The opportunity to help his sister get through university without debt was one he'd *wanted* to take. Now she had the chance to start her life off with a clean slate. Of course, her future-husband would have helped her pay it off...but he didn't want Kayla to feel like the money was a reason to stay with someone. He wanted to know that she wasn't bound out of financial dependence.

Lord knew his mother had experienced that with Kayla's dad. And look how *that* fuck-up had turned out.

"Anyway, I said I would handle it." Beckett didn't want to get into it with his sister tonight, which inevitably ended up happening whenever they talked about their mother. "But I *do* have a favor to ask."

"Sure, what is it?"

"I have a friend who's a makeup artist. I know you're looking for someone to do your wedding makeup and I thought you might be interested in hiring her." He felt like he should add something extra, something to qualify McKenna's skills, but what the hell did he know about makeup? "She's very...professional."

Kind of.

"I'm happy to do a trial with her," Kayla said. "You know I can't say yes simply because she's a friend, but I'm certainly happy to meet with her."

"That's all I'm asking."

"Great. Email me her contact details and I'll call her." Kayla paused. "She wouldn't happen to be the cute woman who lives on your floor, would she?"

"I never said she was cute."

"Right, no. What did you say? Attractive?" His sister

laughed. "That's about as much of a compliment as you'd ever give anyone, so I guess she must be a stunner."

Beckett grunted. It was time to get out of this conversation before Kayla could press for any more details. "I have to go. I'll email you. And leave the mum issue to me, I'll sort something out."

He ended the call and sagged back in his office chair. Life would be so much easier if he could just deal with computers.

• • •

It was only Monday and already Beckett was ready for the week to be over. He'd called JGL Investments to tell them that their offer was bullshit—in not so many words, of course—and that he wasn't going to hand over complete control. This wasn't his first time around with startups, so they weren't going to take him for a ride. Unfortunately, they weren't willing to negotiate.

So that was that. Another possibility biting the dust.

Some small part of him had hoped that they might see reason, which would take the pressure off with everything else. But no such luck. And, since he couldn't pay his coders yet, he needed to keep on doing it himself. Which meant it was unlikely he'd be stopping work before midnight again tonight. So he'd gone to get a coffee from the only spot that was still open at nine p.m., in the hopes some caffeine might perk him back up. As yet, no such luck.

At least he wouldn't need to have the "work/life balance" argument with Sherri today. Small mercies.

Beckett sipped his latte and stared at the flashing number above the elevator doors while he waited. Six…five…four…

"Hi, Beckett," a feminine voice made him snap his head to the side. McKenna.

She wore black jeans and a bright pink coat. Her long

brown and purple hair hung in soft waves, and she smelled like vanilla cupcakes. A pair of impossibly high ankle boots brought her up a few inches closer to him, though he'd still have to bend down to kiss her.

Yeah. Because that's how you judge someone's height? Idiot.

Dammit. Why did the elevators take so long in this building? The thought of being inside that tin can masquerading as a form of transport with her made his fingers twitch. Suddenly the issues with JGL were the least of his worries.

She looked at him expectantly. Oh yeah, she'd made that comment about him always grunting whenever she greeted him.

"Hello, McKenna." He watched the screen count down until it displayed *G* for ground. A second later, the doors slid open and he motioned for her to go ahead of him.

She'd already tapped the first-floor button by the time he stepped in, and they stood at opposite ends of the elevator carriage like two wary animals trying to preserve their personal space. Her eyes darted over to him, her sooty lashes touching as she blinked.

He got the urge to say something and cut through the tension-filled silence to make her stop looking at him like that. Like she wanted…who the hell knew? What did women want, anyway?

But the words wouldn't come. He couldn't seem to find the right thing to say.

So, how does the clitoral stimulator work?

I hope you're enjoying your sex toys.

Perhaps I could have a demonstration?

He almost choked on his own spit. This was *exactly* why he should have stayed the hell away from her instead of agreeing to her deal. For some reason, she seemed to turn his brain—

which he regarded as functioning *well* above average—into nothing more than a useless mound of pudding.

"So…" She rocked back and forth on her boots, the pencil-thin heels making him struggle to swallow. They were covered in little gold studs that seemed to wink mischievously at him. "Crappy weather, huh?"

Beckett made a sound of agreement in the back of his throat.

"You don't—?"

Her words were cut short when the elevator jolted suddenly, its smooth ascent halted with an abrupt jerk and an unhealthy grinding sound. The lights flickered and then went out.

"What the hell?" McKenna squeaked. "Beckett?"

"It's okay," he said calmly. This wasn't the first time the elevator had malfunctioned, and he'd complained to the maintenance manager a few times that they needed more regular servicing. "It'll be working in a minute."

Her breathing cut through the quiet. Without the electric hum of the elevator, his ears tuned in to every little sound. In the pitch black, his other senses were heightened. Awareness prickled along his skin. She was close. So close.

Something brushed his arm and he turned, bumping into the solid warmth of her. The back of his hand met her fingertips and they both pulled away.

"Sorry, I…I don't like the dark," she said breathlessly, speaking over a rustling sound. "Dammit, my phone's dead. I don't suppose you have yours?"

"I left it upstairs," he replied.

"Shit." Her voice wavered.

Bloody hell. The desire to wrap her up in his arms surged through him with the force of a runaway train. He cleared his throat and the sound echoed in the quiet carriage. Touching her wouldn't be appropriate, but he couldn't shake the urge to comfort her. He remembered spending hours sitting on the edge of Kayla's bed, talking her to sleep each night after her father had taken off. She'd hated the dark, too.

"What did you do today?" he asked.

"Just work." Her shaky voice came from right next to him. "And I was getting some business cards printed up for my freelance work. I am *so* ready to be done with retail."

"You're not happy at the department store?"

She made an adorable snorting sound. "As much as I enjoy picking up after customers who have no sense of hygiene when it comes to testers…uh, yeah. I'm a little sick of that place."

"What do the cards look like?"

"Oh, they're really nice." Her voice perked up significantly. "I had a friend design them for me. They're purple and black with silver writing, kind of edgy but still girlie. Like me."

Edgy but still girlie. It was the perfect description.

"It took me ages to pick the right font. Who knew there were so many fonts in the world. I like the loopy ones that kind of look like handwriting, but some of them were hard to read. I think the one I ended up with for my name was called Allure…or was it Allura? Something like that, anyway…"

He found her stream-of-conscious chatter soothing. Which was unusual. Bizarre, even. Normally, after a rough day of work—or in this case, a rough couple of days—Beckett would crave peace and quiet. It had driven Sherri nuts, because she always wanted to debrief. Dissect. Brainstorm. And Beckett simply wanted to throw his headphones on and go for a run. Alone.

But McKenna's voice had a musical quality that lured the trouble of his day away from him.

"And *then* we had to pick a pattern. Stripes or spots. I'm partial to stripes, because I think they're quite chic but apparently that can make it hard to read the words in such a small space. So, we went with polka dots. Not those big ones, but more like delicate little dots. Like the size of a pinhead." A nervous giggle punctuated her sentence. "Sorry, I talk a lot when I'm nervous. That was probably way more detail than you wanted."

Why was she nervous? Was it simply being in the dark, or was it something else?

"I only wanted you to talk so you'd stop worrying," he said. "You can talk about whatever you like."

"Oh, so it's a tactic."

Was it his imagination or did she sound disappointed? "I prefer technique."

"Right." The silence stretched on in the dark for a few heartbeats. "You're a bit of a mystery, you know that?"

He forced down the bubble of annoyance in his throat. McKenna wasn't to know that she'd hit on a sore point of his—but Beckett was sick to death of hearing people say words to that effect. Sherri had hurled something similar at him during more than one fight. Closed off, she'd called him, a total bloody mystery. She'd also had a few other choice words. Impersonal. Impassive. Stoic. A brick wall of a man with a steel gate around his heart.

Better than being like an emotional firework, in his opinion.

He frowned in the darkness. The elevator didn't usually take this long to get going again. The last time it had barely been a minute…and how long had they been here now? Five minutes? Or was it more? None of the buttons were showing up on the control panel.

"I guess I keep to myself," he said.

He wasn't about to tell her that he found relationships to be a minefield. Because someone like her would never understand that.

"Ha, unlike me. I tend to blurt everything out about

myself. Like that time when—" She stopped abruptly when the elevator made a whirring noise and all the lights suddenly flickered back on. "Oh, thank *God*."

His eyes reacted to the sudden influx of light, flinching away from the brightness. Or perhaps they were flinching away from McKenna because her hand had flown to his bicep, and for some reason his skin was doing this weird burning, prickling thing.

"Thanks for not judging me," she said, her tongue darting out to smooth over a plump, pink bottom lip. The shade matched her coat. "I know it's stupid to be scared of the dark as an adult."

"It's not stupid."

The elevator dinged and the doors slid open. For a moment, neither one of them moved. McKenna's eyes tracked his face, as if she was waiting for something.

"After you." He held his arm across the doors to make sure they wouldn't close.

They walked down the hall in companionable silence, and she stopped in front of her door. An invitation hovered on his tongue.

Come to my place. Let's have a drink.

No, he had to keep his eye on the prize. His brain, at least, knew the score. As for his body…well, the way McKenna looked at him had some tension building behind the fly of his jeans. Her eyes seemed to comb him over, stoking embers burning in his chest, encouraging them to catch alight.

"I told Kayla about you, by the way," he said, hoping that if he kept his brain moving, then his body might calm the hell down.

"You did!" She clapped her hands together. "Why didn't you lead off with that? That would *definitely* have distracted me in the elevator."

Truth be told, the second he saw McKenna pretty much

everything else had flown out of his head. She had a very annoying way of making that happen. Beckett shrugged.

"And?" McKenna blinked at him incredulously. "What did she say? Don't leave me hanging."

"She asked for your details and said she would call you."

A high-pitched squeal shot out of McKenna's mouth and she grabbed his arm again. Why did she keep doing that? More importantly, why did it make his throat feel all tight?

"That's great!" Her eyes sparked.

"It's not a guarantee that she'll hire you."

"I know. But my work will speak for itself."

There was a time bomb ticking in his chest and whenever she got close it felt like the countdown sped up, inching him closer to trouble. To doing something stupid like asking her over to have a drink with him. Or worse, giving in to the fantasy raging in his head that was yelling at him to push her hard against her front door and lower his head to hers.

"Well, good night," he said suddenly before turning on his heel and heading toward his apartment.

"Good night." Her voice floated behind him. She sounded confused.

Ugh. The quicker he got into his apartment the better. He needed all the distance he could get, though something told him that a couple of apartments between them wouldn't be enough. If he wanted any chance of keeping his head in the game—and keeping his focus on solving his current problem—he needed to keep face-to-face contact to a minimum.

"Wait!" she called out, the sound of her footsteps quickening behind him. "We need to have dinner."

"Dinner?"

"Yeah." She stopped short. Was it his imagination or were her cheeks a little pinker than before?

"Why?"

"To discuss how we're going to get your fiancée back."

"Why does that require dinner?" The thought of sitting down for an evening with McKenna unnerved him. The scene in the elevator was bad enough, how would he keep his head straight for more than ten minutes around her?

"People often discuss business over dinner." She smiled. "Tomorrow night, meet me at Wentworth on Bourke Street at six."

He frowned. This was courting disaster. He couldn't seem to hang on to his usual logical state around her. So that meant he needed to keep interactions to a minimum. Risk management, that's what it was. "Can't we just do it over email?"

"No," she said, looking at him as if he'd suddenly started talking gibberish. "This is a personal problem, and I know I won't get the information I need over email. Six p.m. sharp." She whirled around and headed to her apartment without giving him time to protest.

So much for keeping his distance.

Chapter Five

McKenna stared intently at the lash line of her client, carefully dragging an angled brush coated with black gel liner to create the perfect flick at the corner of her eye. She leaned back to take in the bigger picture, her gaze sweeping from one eye to the other. They matched. Perfectly.

"I usually press a little black shadow over the top of the liquid liner to set it in place," McKenna said as she dipped her brush into a pan of inky shadow appropriately called *Jet*. "Just be sure to tap the brush and remove any excess. You don't want dark shadow falling onto your cheeks because it can be a real pain to remove."

The client sat patiently with her eyes closed while McKenna put the finishing touches on her special date-night makeup. Friday afternoons were usually back-to-back with city workers on their way to parties and events. It was the best part of McKenna's week, since she got to spend more time applying makeup than selling it. Although, she still had a quota to meet. Which meant a little *would you like fries with that* action.

"I'd definitely recommend a matte formulation for the black shadow. It'll help the liner look more striking and it also comes in handy if you want to create a smoky look." She studied the makeup with a critical eye, brushing a cotton bud over a tiny dot of mascara that had transferred from her client's lashes. "The shimmery blacks don't have the same punch. I'm sure we've got a matte one left if in stock, so I can put it with the rest of your purchases. Here, let's see what you think."

The client opened her eyes and her mouth hung open in a surprised *O* as she peered into the small mirror that McKenna was holding up. "I love it!"

Those three words never failed to make McKenna's chest warm with pride. The big reveal was the best moment of a makeup artist's day. Seeing the joy and confidence radiating from her clients' faces made all the crappy bits—like sales targets and dodgy returns and lectures from her boss—feel worth it.

"I feel like I could never master the winged liner." The client sighed. "Can't you live at my house and do this for me every morning?"

"You'd be surprised how often people ask me that." McKenna grinned. "But practice makes perfect and there's always makeup wipes if things don't go according to plan."

She grouped the products together into categories—base, eyes, and lips. It was part of the CAM-Ready Cosmetics selling procedure. Never assume the client is only going to buy one product, because you might lose a sale.

"Now, I know you mentioned that you wanted to take the lipstick and gloss for touch-ups tonight. But I definitely recommend grabbing one of the gel liners and black shadow so you can practice at home." She held up her angled brush. "A brush like this will be easiest because you can fit it against the lash line and 'stamp' the wing into place. It's what I used when I first learned how to do winged liner."

"Okay, you got me." The client shook her head ruefully. "I'll take it all. My credit card will hate me, but at least I'm having fun. Right?"

"Exactly. Makeup is meant to be fun. Stay here and I'll go get everything."

As she was scurrying around the store, excusing herself to squeeze between customers so should could get to the drawers containing the stock, she spied a male figure.

Beckett.

He stood at the edge of the retail chaos, hands shoved into his pockets, legs crossed at the ankles. Looking like a freaking GQ model in suit pants instead of his usual jeans. A white shirt was tucked in and open at the collar, the sleeves rolled up to reveal a heavy silver watch. A neat tan belt accentuated his trim waist.

Their moment in the elevator was still fresh in her mind. The way he spoke to her in the pitch-black, his tone soothing and warm. The easy way he'd taken control of the situation—of making her relax—was enough to get her knees wobbling. The air had been filled with that snap, crackle, and pop of tension she knew to be rare. She'd used up every last drop of willpower not to reach for him in the anonymity of the dark.

Ducking her head, she opened the drawer containing the lipsticks. Rows upon rows of neat black boxes stared back at her, the tiny font of the shade names swimming as her eyes failed to focus. She knew Beckett was coming to meet her after work so they could discuss the particulars of their deal. So why was she shocked?

What if it wasn't shock? That pulse-racing, dry-mouthed feeling might be a symptom of something else.

You've agreed to help him get his ex back. That makes him the very definition of the wrong guy to lust over.

If only her lady bits would listen to her brain. The brain

was smart, the lady bits…well, not so much. And for some reason they remained disconnected, despite McKenna's attempts to get them on the same page.

She cashed her customer out, slipping a few samples into her bag with a cheeky wink, knowing the woman would be delighted. Then she stood at the register, waiting for her daily summary report to print out so she could scrawl her tally on the piece of paper in their day folder. Two hundred dollars over her target, with an average Items Per Sale of 1.95. Not bad at all. She bid her team a farewell and grabbed her bag from the lockers out back before making her way through the store, her eyes immediately zeroing in on where Beckett stood.

"Hey." She held up her hand in greeting.

He nodded. "Hello."

"No grunting today, very good." A cheeky grin spread over her lips. "I guess that means you're getting comfortable with me, huh?"

"Don't get used to it."

As usual, she couldn't tell if he was joking. Perhaps she'd try to work that into their plans—after all, clear communication was good for relationships. At least, that's what she'd been told by people who managed to not get dumped every few months.

"So I thought we could grab a drink and bite to eat at Ca de Vin." She hitched her bag higher on her shoulder as they walked through the Wentworth Department store's front doors and out onto bustling Bourke Street. "It's just here and I'm starving."

"I forget to eat when I'm working, too," he said.

McKenna had to stifle a laugh. Forgetting to eat wasn't something that happened to her—being on her feet all day at work helped her maintain a healthy appetite. And she had a reputation for snacking. No bag of chips or chocolate bar was ever safe around her.

They headed into Ca de Vin and were seated at a small table against a wall. The restaurant itself was the epitome of Melbourne dining—stuck between two buildings in what used to be an alleyway, some industrious person had slapped a tarp over the top and voila! Instant restaurant. The city was like that—if there was an unused nook, someone would find a way to serve food there.

"This looks like we're on a date," Beckett said, his brows creased.

He had a point. The table was intimate, meaning they were seated close to one another. And a single tea light candle flickered inside a glass, giving off a warm orange glow.

"So what?"

"It *isn't* a date," he said.

McKenna rolled her eyes. "I am aware of that. Especially given we're here to discuss how to get your girl back. Now I'm going to stop you before you accidentally insult me by assuming I want you, because I don't."

Liar, liar, pants on fire.

His blue eyes raked over her in a way that made it difficult for her to swallow. "I wasn't going to say that."

"Good. And I doubt anyone will assume we're together because it's not like there's any chemistry." Her traitorous mind flashed back to that moment in front of her door, where she'd been at risk of bursting into flames from his stare alone. "You're not my type."

Operation Self-Love step one: set boundaries to avoid self-sabotage.

"What's your type?" His head tilted slightly.

McKenna picked up a menu and pretended to inspect the drink options while she grappled for a response. What *was* her type? "Men who are wrong for me."

Dammit. This wasn't the time to be telling the truth.

Beckett ran a hand along his jaw as though giving her statement serious thought. "So you have bad taste in men?"

"No need to kick a girl while she's down, buddy." McKenna pursed her lips. "But yes, I may have some trouble picking men who have long-term staying power. Not exactly my fault, most men aren't looking to stick around and the older they get, the better they are at hiding those intentions."

Her track record showed a sad inability to learn from her mistakes. She seemed to aim too high or too low, picking men who either missed the mark on her relationship dreams or the ones who labeled her a good-time girl. Where was her Goldilocks of men? Was it so damn impossible to find a guy who had a decent job, wanted to be in a committed relationship, *and* gave her the jittery feeling that only came with good chemistry? Surely that wasn't too much to ask.

The waiter delivered a basket of bread to the table and took their orders. When he left, McKenna reached for a chunk and dunked it into a little dish containing oil and balsamic vinegar. "Besides, why do you care? We're here to discuss *your* relationship failures, not mine."

A flash of emotion streaked across Beckett's face, but it was gone before she could figure out exactly what it meant. "I haven't failed."

"Call it a temporary setback, then. Whatever helps you sleep at night." McKenna chewed. "So, have you figured out why you got dumped yet? That would be useful information to have."

• • •

Beckett got the distinct feeling that McKenna was trying to wind him up on purpose. Though why, he had no idea. He was destined to never understand the female mind, hence why he'd agreed to accept McKenna's help. *She* would give him the insight he needed…once she stopped verbally poking him with a stick, that was.

"I think it was a combination of things."

"Which were…?"

"She thinks I work too much and that I don't pay enough attention to her, for starters. She would always complain that we never went on enough holidays and that I spent too much time with my family." He poured them both a glass of water. "Is that enough to go on?"

"She thinks you spend too much time with your family?" McKenna raised a brow.

"Apparently."

Beckett had dinner once a week like clockwork with his mother and sister. The tradition had started when he'd moved out, because he still wanted to keep an eye on Kayla. She took her father's comings and goings hard, and Beckett didn't want her to think he was abandoning her, too.

"I invited Sherri a few times, but she said she felt like she was encroaching."

"So she would have preferred you to not go at all." She made a little noise of annoyance, but the waiter arrived before she could continue.

The guy was about Beckett's age, with dark hair and olive skin. He had a slight Italian accent and stared at McKenna appreciatively as he announced the dishes, turning her from prickly interrogator to giggling flirt in less than a second. She all but batted her lashes at the guy, laughing sweetly at his jokes. For some reason that made a tight ball of tension gather in Beckett's stomach.

For all the waiter knew, they *were* on a date. And as uncomfortable as he'd been with McKenna's needy gaze on him the night they got stuck in the elevator, it felt even worse when she directed it at someone else.

"I don't know," Beckett said after they'd ordered their

meals. "She seemed to be under the impression I should know what she wants at all times, even though she's not always very forthcoming with information."

Beckett sighed. It seemed to be a game that Sherri played with him—sometimes he got it right and was rewarded with her blissful smile. Other times he missed the mark, and bore the brunt of her cold shoulder for days at a time. He'd never quite figured out how to tip the odds his way.

But he shouldn't be telling McKenna all this. Their issues were private, and it was only right to pass on what McKenna needed in order to help him.

"I do work a lot, though," he admitted. "I get absorbed by my job."

"You like what you do, huh?" McKenna smiled. "I'm like that, too. Sometimes when I'm working on a face chart I block out the rest of the world."

"What's a face chart?"

Her eyes lit up. "Oh, it's a map of the face that makeup artists use to plan out a look. We sketch out the design and fill it in using makeup products so when we need to recreate the look we have an exact guide of what to do."

They paused as the waiter arrived with their food.

"So what's your plan, Miss *I'm an excellent matchmaker*?" He drove a fork into his ravioli. "How do I fix this problem?"

"I need to figure out the situation before I devise a plan. No point jumping the gun, because you'll only get one shot at this." She twirled her spaghetti around her fork. "I need to understand why she left."

"I told you, she didn't say anything. She just…left."

He'd been a little dumfounded, since her usual departures had been accompanied by lots of bluster and yelling. This time he didn't even have the chance to argue, she'd already had her bags packed by the time he returned home from his meeting, and she'd walked past him without a word.

"You told me what her complaints were," she said. "And women don't always say exactly what they mean. You have to read between the lines."

"Maybe they'd have a better chance of getting what they want if they came out and asked for it," he grumbled. "I'm not a bloody mind reader."

"In any case, *I* know why she left, because I know how women think." She set her cutlery down as though about to make a very important announcement. "She thinks you don't love her."

"Because I work hard and make time for my family?" he scoffed.

"Because you don't make her your top priority." She looked far too smug for her own good. "She probably feels like she's playing second fiddle to a whole host of other things, like work and other people in your life."

"Those things are important to me." His voice came out a little sharper than he'd intended, but this picking apart of his personal life was like having needles stuck into his skin.

After growing up the local "charity case" in his middle-class suburb—where everyone knew his family's troubles—he craved privacy. It was his shield from the world. His protection. Because it allowed him to be anyone he wanted—so he'd chosen the path of an entrepreneur, where a little mystery was a good thing. But McKenna's comments and questions were like tiny hammers against his outer shell, and the feeling of her trying to get closer vibrated through his body.

"Of course they are. But you're a workaholic, right? You said yourself that you work a lot."

"I'm working on a startup. Being a workaholic is in the job description." Beckett forced his shoulders to relax, as they were bunching around his neck the way they usually did when he felt defensive. "Look, you want to start you own business so surely you understand. It takes hard work to get something off the ground."

"Oh, I understand." She bobbed her head, her dangling earrings making tinkling sounds. "But you work long hours, right? What time do you usually finish up at night?"

Beckett speared another ravioli. He couldn't remember the last time he'd logged off before midnight. It'd been months. Some nights he didn't even make it to bed, because he only had enough energy to collapse on his couch.

Okay, so maybe McKenna was onto something. "It depends," he said. "I work until the job is done."

"That's a fallacy." She offered a knowing smile. "Because the job is never done, is it?"

"No, it's not," he admitted. But the job *wouldn't* be done unless he started taking action. In his experience, talk was cheap…and pointless. "Have we finished with the Dr. Phil portion of this meeting? Because I'd really like to know what the next steps are."

McKenna stifled a smile. "Step number one is to stop treating this like a business transaction. Personal relationships aren't always logical, trust me. If you're going to do this, then you need to loosen up a bit."

"Do I not seem relaxed?" He raked a hand through his hair, unsure how to deal with the bubbling frustration that was slowly swelling within him. All he could think about was how much work he had to do—and how delectable McKenna's mouth looked as she pushed each forkful of food between her lips—neither of which were helpful.

"I've seen politicians in the middle of media scandals who looked more relaxed than you." She laughed. "You're uptight in a cute, Clark Kent meets Christian Grey kind of way. I'll be honest, I dig it. But the first thing I'm going to do is teach you how to relax and enjoy a date."

Questions ran through his brain like a bunch of toddlers high on sugar. He couldn't even begin to unpack her comments—she thought he was cute? She wanted to teach him how to relax...on a date? And who the hell was Christian Grey?

"How exactly do you plan to do that?" he asked, shoving the rest of the questions aside.

"You're going to go on a date with me and I'm going to critique you." She grinned. "Think of it as me beta-testing your dating skills."

"You're kidding me." He couldn't even begin to list all the things wrong with that scenario. But right there, at the very top of the pile, was the rush of satisfaction knowing that he'd get to be with her alone again. And that was a very, very bad sign.

"Nope." She reached for her water and sipped, leaving behind a perfect imprint of hot pink lipstick. "Not even a little bit."

"Fine." He nodded, digesting the information. "A test date it is."

He didn't like the self-satisfied look on her face, that subtle little smirk that told him she thought he'd fail. Beckett didn't like failing, so he certainly wasn't going to give her that satisfaction. If she wanted the date to end all dates, then he was going to give it to her.

Chapter Six

"Wait, wait, wait." Emery held up her hands as she perched, feet tucked under her, on a stool. "You're going on a date with this guy? What happened to Operation Self-Love?"

Emery, her sister Isla, and McKenna had gathered for their weekly wine and bitch session. They rotated hosting duties, and tonight the three girls were lounging around Isla's immaculate kitchen. A spread of veggies, dips, cheeses, crackers, and chocolates were artfully arranged—as was Isla's style. Two bottles of wine were open, but Emery had opted for a boutique beer, which she gestured with as she spoke.

"I thought you were trying to help him get his ex back," she added.

"It's a test date," McKenna clarified. "So I can really see what's going on. If I'm going to have any chance of helping him, I need to know what his flaws are. Well, other than being a workaholic."

Isla leaned on the kitchen counter, propping herself up on her elbows. "Any guesses?"

"He's a bit of a mystery," she said, reaching for a celery

stick and dunking it into a bowl of homemade hummus. "Definitely an introvert, which normally I wouldn't like. But he's got this strong, silent thing going on that's quite yummy."

"Why does it matter whether you like him if this is just a test date?" Emery asked.

"It doesn't." McKenna busied herself with cutting the wheel of camembert into six perfect pieces. "I'm just saying…"

"Self-love not all it's cracked up to be?" Emery cackled. "Screw the ex. Maybe you should take him for a 'test drive' as well."

"Emery!" Isla shook her head in a disappointed mother hen way. "McKenna is doing something good for herself. There's nothing wrong with taking some time alone to figure out what you want in life."

"Not the advice I was expecting from Mrs. Loved-up Wifey To-Be." Emery took a long draw on her beer. "I thought you were pro commitment."

Isla huffed. "I'm anti settling."

"For the record, I know *exactly* what I want." McKenna sighed. "That's part of the problem. Reality is not matching up to my expectations. Hence why I'm fine going on a fake date."

"So where is he taking you?" Isla asked.

"I have no idea. I told him to set it up so I can see how creative he is. All I know is we're meeting after work Wednesday night."

The truth wasn't quite so cut and dry as that. McKenna hadn't initially planned the whole test-date thing in advance. But having dinner with Beckett—watching him glare at the waiter when she'd flirted with him and hearing that he made time weekly for his family—was a little too enjoyable. Why shouldn't she get some personal benefit out of this arrangement? And a fake date was the only kind she was allowed during Operation Self-Love.

Though keeping her end of the bargain might be tougher than she expected. McKenna had a pretty good idea what had gone wrong in Beckett and Sherri's relationship—it was the same reason McKenna was still single. Expectations.

They were good to have, but they also caused problems. She didn't want to settle for a deadbeat, but it seemed the serious guys didn't want to settle for her. And she'd put money on the fact that Sherri wanted hearts and flowers and romance, while Beckett wanted someone who understood and supported his drive and ambition.

Yeah, expectations could be a contrary bitch like that.

"So what's the criteria?" Emery rustled around in a bag of corn chips and pulled out a handful, dropping crumbs all around her in the process. Isla frowned and reached for a tissue to wipe them up. "Are there any instant fail sections? Like if he clips a roundabout?"

"I see you're still going with the whole driving test thing," McKenna said drily. "No instant fails. But I want to see how he goes setting a date up, if he's attentive and engaged, if he makes me feel special. I suspect his ex was looking for a little more romance but Beckett is…well, he seems like a very logical guy. So maybe I can give him a few pointers for the grovel."

"The grovel?" Isla raised a brow.

"You know, that bit at the end of a chick flick where the guy is all 'I made a terrible mistake not treating you right' and then they kiss and she does the foot-pop thing."

Emery shook her head. "The foot-pop thing?"

McKenna rolled her eyes. "Haven't you watched *The Princess Diaries* or like any other rom com made in the last two decades?"

"Uh, no, because Anne Hathaway is the spawn of the devil and I don't hate myself." Emery munched on her corn chips.

Isla shook her head. "You hate everything romantic."

"It's the way of the man-repeller." Emery winked.

McKenna's friends dissolved into an argument about the merit of chick flicks and she went to pour herself another glass of wine. As she reached for a fresh bottle, her phone buzzed. These days, especially when she was already with her besties, that was a rare occurrence. Which could only mean one thing...

Mother.

Or rather, her mother's assistant. The formidable Mrs. Jones, a woman whom McKenna was certain had come out of the womb wearing a twinset and a disapproving frown. Her first word had likely been *no.*

Evil Jones: Your mother requests your presence at the family home for dinner next week, Thursday night. 7p.m. sharp. Smart casual.

Smart freaking casual? Honestly, who required a dress code for a family dinner...at home, no less.

McKenna: So that's a no to booty shorts, then?

Evil Jones: Don't be smart.

McKenna snorted. No chance of that, at least not where her family was concerned. They had three doctors, one lawyer, and her, the lowly retail worker. A.k.a the black sheep. Just freaking great.

At least her faux-date with Beckett would give her something to look forward to. She'd been planning to wear her sparkly dress on their outing, but that might now have to be saved for the family dinner.

Sequins were smart casual, right?

McKenna rolled her eyes and tapped at her phone.

McKenna: Don't worry, I've got the perfect outfit already picked out.

• • •

Beckett raked his hand through his hair for what must have been the hundredth time that afternoon, while he waited for McKenna to show up. They were supposed to meet in the foyer of their building. But she was already ten minutes late.

He frowned. Perhaps he should have brought his laptop down with him. Ten minutes could be used to achieve quite a lot—he could have answered some emails, or tweaked that one line of code that was bugging him. He could have approved the graphics his designer had sent over, or worked on his beta testing release schedule. Or he could have even—

"Beckett?" McKenna waved her hand in front of his face, blinding him with her neon-pink nails. "Oh, you *are* awake. I thought you might have been in some weird open-eye sleep trance."

He pushed up from the foyer's couch. "Definitely awake."

It would be hard not to be wide-awake around McKenna, not only because she was gorgeous but because she seemed to enjoy wearing shades of the retina-searing variety. Usually coupled with something sparkly. Beckett briefly wondered if looking at her clothing had the same effect on the brain as looking at a screen before bedtime.

He zeroed in on the purple leopard print book in her hands, which had a pen attached with a black ribbon. "Why are you holding a notebook?"

"How else am I going to take notes for the review?" Her tinkling laughter ran right through him, like the sound had somehow hitched a ride on the blood pumping through his veins.

It left him with a most unusual humming sensation that

was equally pleasant and foreign.

"Review?" He raised a brow.

"Well, this *is* a test date. I'm sure you'd want some feedback at the end so you can understand how to improve, right?"

Beckett wasn't so sure about that. He'd never been the kind of guy to crave praise. In fact, he much preferred to know in his gut that he'd done a good job rather than hear it from someone else. However, he *had* struck a deal with McKenna and if this was her method of helping him get Sherri back, then so be it. Any discomfort from listening to her pick apart his approach would be well worth it when he got his life back on track.

After speaking to his mother today—who was adamant that she was in the right and, as such, had *not* gotten her job back—he really needed to make sure things were smoothed over with Sherri and her father. Quickly and for good.

"That was a rhetorical question, in case you wondered." McKenna smiled sweetly, but Beckett had the feeling there was a tough interior beneath her *My Little Pony* packaging. "Don't worry, I won't be harsh."

"My feelings don't bruise easily," he replied.

"Good to know you have them," she said with a wink. "I wasn't so sure."

"Do you think I'm a robot or something?"

"Well, it's just that..." She tilted her head as if trying to figure out exact what she wanted to say. "You don't seem awfully cut up about losing Sherri."

"I've entered into an agreement that goes against my personal way of doing business in order to get your help in winning her back. How does that show a lack of feeling?"

"Oh boy." She sucked in a breath. "I don't even know where to start with that."

He thought about standing there and arguing with her

that a lack of outward emotion didn't necessarily represent a lack of inward emotion, but he wasn't willing to get docked points before they'd even started. While he might not need praise, he didn't want to fail her test, either.

But what was it about women who refused to believe that he felt something simply because he wasn't doing a Hallmark-style declaration?

"How about we start with the date?" He looked at his watch. "We're already behind schedule."

"You got somewhere else to be?" She cocked a brow.

"No, but I don't want to miss our reservation."

McKenna's large blue eye sparkled. "In that case, let's go. Lead the way."

Suddenly Beckett's frustration was replaced by an entirely new sensation—a kind of churning, acidic anxiousness that wasn't as unpleasant as it sounded. He reached for McKenna's arm and she readily handed it over, a smile blooming on her lips that told him he'd scored a point.

He glanced at McKenna's outfit. Originally he'd planned for them to walk the ten minutes to the restaurant, since it wasn't raining for once. But her legs were only covered in a set of sheer black stockings and she'd worn a pair of heels that looked more suited to skewering a steak than a romantic stroll.

Or should that be, skewering a man's heart?

Let's not forget this is nothing but a drill.

So why didn't his body's automatic reactions seem to understand that? He had a sudden need to impress her. To wow her.

You just want to past the test. Totally normal for an ambitious Type-A person. Totally 100 percent normal.

Instead of exiting through the front entrance, Beckett steered her toward the elevator that would take them to the underground garage. As they walked, her nearness overwhelmed him. McKenna was just…so much. She smelled like dessert—sugar and peaches and vanilla ice cream—sweetly cloying in the best way possible. And the warmth from her shoulder brushing his arm made his cotton shirt feel as though it was about to burn up and disintegrate right off his body.

"You look lovely," he said as they stepped into the elevator. "I like the…fringy things on your eyes."

She beamed. "Thanks. They're faux mink false lashes, actually. I bought them because I saw this girl on YouTube review them. They're just as soft as the real mink but, you know, without the potential for animal cruelty. I was a vegetarian for a while but…"

McKenna prattled cheerfully as they dropped down to the basement and walked to the spot where his Mercedes was housed. He'd never met anyone in his whole life who talked as much as she did, but he never felt pressure to talk back. In fact, she seemed quite happy to tell him all about her flirtations with being a vegetarian, then a pescetarian, and that she loved CAM-Ready cosmetics because they were cruelty-free.

The upbeat tone of her voice soothed rather than irritated him. Perhaps it was because he could stay quiet without facing accusations of being disinterested.

"So, where are you taking me?" She slid into the passenger seat and pulled the seatbelt across her middle.

Beckett swallowed. A moment ago, when she'd been standing, her black leather skirt hadn't seemed that short. But now, extra inches of her stocking-covered legs had been exposed to his hungry eyes. A chunky silver tab dangled over her thigh, the zipper itself extending all the way up to her waist. He wondered what it would be like to slide the tab up and watch her be exposed.

He cleared his throat and focused his attention on

steering them out to the street. "Tide Pool."

"Fancy." She bobbed her head. "We probably could have walked."

"I thought you would be cold." His gaze dropped to her legs again. "That's a very short skirt."

McKenna bristled. "I'm not sure whether to be annoyed at your judging tone or happy that you were concerned about my comfort."

Beckett stopped himself from correcting her; he wasn't being judgmental at all. But it was probably better that she thought that rather than know the truth—that the thoughts about what lay underneath her skirt had gotten him all tongue-tied and…horny.

What the hell was wrong with him? He'd always hated those guys who thought with their dicks instead of their heads. Yet now, in her presence, he was at very real risk of losing his head…the important one.

"I guess that's up to you," he said finally. "I can't tell you what to think."

Out of the corner of his eye, he noticed her studying him. "I can't figure you out, Beckett Walsh. Are you so honest that you come across blunt, or are you just an asshole?" She sounded genuinely puzzled.

Ouch. "I suppose if you're asking that question then this date isn't off to a very good start."

It wasn't the first time someone had called him blunt. In business he didn't mind it so much, but in his personal life he supposed it probably wasn't the best way to be. There was such a fine line between bluntness and honesty that he wasn't sure exactly where to step all the time.

Like most things about dealing with people, it was not as black and white as he would have preferred.

"I don't *try* to be an asshole," he added.

She laughed. "How about I start taking notes once we

arrive? That'll give you a fresh start."

He palmed the steering wheel, pulling the car slowly into the valet entrance of the Crown Entertainment complex. Within minutes they were at the restaurant, which Sherri had talked about numerous times. It had required some schedule juggling in order to get a reservation. But if McKenna wanted to see what he could do—then he'd give her the best.

A maître d' led them through the dimly lit restaurant, which had a modern yet intimate atmosphere. It was certainly a lot fancier than the places he usually preferred to dine, which were more of the ma and pa home-style meal varieties. In fact, when McKenna had first suggested the date he'd thought about taking her to this little place out in Carlton where the family's matriarch still ran the kitchen—with an iron fist, he'd heard—and they made the best Gorgonzola gnocchi. But it wasn't "gold star" worthy—at least, Sherri hadn't been too impressed the one time he'd taken her there.

"Well, I certainly feel like a princess," McKenna said as they took their seats. Their coats had been whisked away, and now her skin was playing peek-a-boo with a slinky top that had cut-outs at the shoulders.

"You haven't been here before?" he asked.

"I have." She nodded, sucking on her lower lip for a moment. "My parents eat out a lot because they both work such long hours, and my dad's office is just up on Bourke Street."

"What do they do?"

She wrinkled her nose. "Dad's a name partner in his law firm. Mum's a GP and has a clinic with her business partner in East Melbourne."

In other words, McKenna came from money. For some reason, that surprised him. He supposed she might not be filthy rich, but certainly her family would be well off enough that she shouldn't need to beg and bargain for work. More than that, McKenna struck him as incredibly humble. Not to say that all wealthy people weren't humble…but it seemed to be a less common quality, in his experience.

"Both my brothers are doctors, too." She rolled her eyes. "Guess what that makes me?"

"The creative one."

A grin crept across her face. "Good answer."

She flipped open her notebook and scribbled something down. The gold details on the pen flashed in the lighting as he tried to read her handwriting. But in the dimness, her flowery, looping cursive was hard to discern.

"No peeking," she said, looking up. "I'll give you a rundown at the end of the night."

They flipped through the menu, and Beckett ordered a bottle of wine to be brought to the table. He tried not to think of his monetary issues as he ordered, rather looking at it as an investment in a solution. It was that mode of thinking that had gotten him to take a number of financial risks that had paid off during his career. Though somehow, as he watched McKenna study the menu with her tongue poking out the corner of her mouth, he wondered if his wallet was really the thing most at risk.

"What do your parents do?" she asked without looking up.

"My mother is a supermarket cashier," he replied, cringing a little at the white lie. But after hearing what her family did, he didn't want to say his mother was willfully unemployed. "And my father passed away when I was a baby. He was an engineer."

Apparently that's where Beckett got his too-quick, too-logical brain from, according to his mother. She didn't always mean it as a compliment, but Beckett took it as one anyway. It made him feel like his father had left something behind for him.

"Oh, I'm so sorry to hear that." McKenna looked up, her brow crinkled. "That must have been tough on you and your sister."

"Well, he's my father. Not hers."

Kayla's father was a whole other kettle of fish—a paternal Houdini who always cared more for himself than he did for his daughter or the mother of his child. He'd drift in and out as he pleased, wreaking havoc on Kayla's hopes for a happy family every damn time.

Beckett's hands clenched under the table. "And he's not worth talking about."

"Duly noted." She bobbed her head. "I won't be nosy."

It wasn't that he wanted to torpedo the conversation, but his family was a touchy subject at the moment. Especially with the added stress of his mother and her job situation… not to mention Kayla's assessment about him enabling her weighing on him like a bag of bricks.

Who was he kidding? His family was a touchy subject all the time. Beckett's need for privacy seemed to bug a lot of people, but McKenna wasn't giving him a hard time. Thankfully.

"You still with me?" she asked, cocking her head. "You've got that glazed-over, cogs turning kind of look."

"I'm still here."

He wasn't sure what else to say. But the soft-eyed look she gave him relieved any pressure in his chest. She wasn't going to pry. Wasn't going to poke and prod until it felt like he'd need to storm off to get the space he needed.

"I was thinking we could get some oysters to start," he said. "I know this is a test date, but I figured an aphrodisiac couldn't hurt."

He flipped the cover closed on his menu and reached for his wine. For a guy who'd grown up loving tests, he felt *way* out of his depth.

Chapter Seven

An aphrodisiac couldn't hurt?

Lord. McKenna would bet her right shoe—which was a Jimmy Choo, and therefore something that would have to be pried out of her cold, dead hands—that an aphrodisiac *would* bloody well hurt right now.

The last thing she needed was to be any more infatuated with this complicated, sexy man. The man who called her eyelashes "fringy things" and was concerned about her walking in the cold and who talked about his family like they were the most precious things in the world. All in the fewest words possible.

Not to mention he'd worn a charcoal suit to dinner with an open-collared white shirt and had clearly done something to his wavy blond hair. Hot. As. Freaking. Hell.

And the man wanted to make her eat something that was going to chemically charge her brain into thinking even *more* about sex? Risky. But what could she say? If she said no without explanation he might wonder why…might suspect that she had a thing for him, which would make it awkward. Or she could claim a shellfish allergy? Oysters came in shells…but were they classed as shellfish for allergy purposes? Also risky.

And, if she claimed to be grossed out by what was essentially snot from the sea…well, that would make her look unworldly. At least, that's what her father had said the one time she'd turned her nose up at them.

"Oysters sound great," she said. Did her voice sound a little squeakier than usual?

Get it together, Prescott. Operation Self-Love is full steam ahead.

At this rate, between Beckett and the oysters, Mr. Whopper was going to get lucky tonight. Operation Self-Love, indeed.

The waiter arrived to take their order, and Beckett motioned for McKenna to go first. When the waiter asked her if she wanted the oysters au natural—their specialty—she agreed. Why not? If she was going to jump in with two feet, then she might as well jump off the highest cliff.

Wait? That wasn't a good thing, was it?

"So…" She toyed with the fancy cutlery, grappling for something to help her focus. "Tell me more about Sherri."

Getting him talking about the girl of his dreams should stop her crazy abstinence-induced lust. Nothing like hearing about the woman who'd snagged a guy like Beckett to make her lady parts shut the hell up.

"What do you want to know?" he asked. His expression was guarded, and his light eyes were like Fort Knox.

"Anything." She shrugged. "How did you meet?"

"At a bar." He reached for his wine.

God. It was like pulling teeth. "Why were you at the bar?"

"I was there after an investor dropped out of a project." He let out a small, sharp laugh. "Drowning my sorrows."

"And in walked the girl of your dreams," McKenna added.

A little flurry of jealousy zipped up her throat—she remembered exactly what Sherri looked like. Blond. Polished. Classy. Not an errant sequin or speck of glitter to be found. Why did guys *always* want someone like that? Someone who was the opposite of McKenna?

Beckett raised a brow. "I don't know if she walked in at that exact moment."

She rolled her eyes. "I didn't mean literally that second."

"I'm a literal guy." A smile quirked on his lips as the oysters arrived at their table.

"You don't say." She shook her head. "I think I've met instruction manuals who were less literal than you."

"And how did you meet them?" he teased. "In a bar?"

"Very funny." She picked up the tiny fork that accompanied their first course and pointed it at him. "You shouldn't be mocking your date judge."

"You're a judge now?" His eyes flicked over her in a way that was somehow both deeply assessing and pleasurable. "I thought you were here to help me."

"We're here to help each other," she corrected, eyeing the oysters like they were some kind of foreign species.

Dammit. Why had she agreed to eat these slimy things?

"Something wrong with the food?" Beckett asked.

"They're just kind of…ugly." She cocked her head. "I've made zombies that were better looking than those things."

And of course, by zombies, she was referring to the special effects kind she'd mastered during her makeup certificate. Not the real kind. *That* would pose a whole new set of problems.

Beckett chuckled, the sound warming her on in the inside like a good Scotch down the back of her throat. "Speaking of which," he said, reaching for an oyster. "Kayla mentioned she's free next week and would love to meet you. I think she's going to email you her details tomorrow."

McKenna breathed a tiny sigh of relief. "Excellent."

Now all she had to do was wow Beckett's sister. No biggie. Most brides wanted the same thing—for you to spend an hour doing their makeup so it looked like they were wearing nothing at all.

She understood the reasoning, but it was so not her style. Give her rhinestone-studded false eyelashes any day of the week. When McKenna eventually found the right man, she was going to wear the biggest false lashes anyone had ever seen. If she didn't send a breeze through the church every time she blinked then they wouldn't be big enough.

"They're not going to bite," Beckett said, nodding to the oysters.

Right. Snotty fish time. "I'm mentally preparing myself." She reached for a shell and held it over the plate toward Beckett. "Cheers."

He clinked his oyster shell against hers with an amused smile. Then he reached for the little fork. Without trying to give away that she had absolutely no idea how to eat an oyster, she pretended to inspect it. That's what people did with wine, right? See. Sniff. Swirl? Dammit, she should have paid more attention at those shitty upper-crust events her mother and father had dragged her to when she was younger.

She picked up the little fork and watched as he used his to loosen the oyster from the shell. Right, so the little buggers were attached. Then he lifted the shell to his mouth and let the oyster slide in. He chewed a little and swallowed, the muscles in his throat working in a way that had her mouth running dry.

How did he make this look so freaking sexy?

When his eyes caught hers, making her feel shivery all over, she quickly brought the fork to her oyster. She gave the oyster a wiggle, but it didn't seem to come loose. Beckett's gaze was on her, she could feel the weight of it. Like all those times her parents' rich, snobby friends had watched her fumble with which damn fork was the salad fork…as if salad was *so* important it needed its own special damn fork.

Stupid freaking salad.

She jabbed the oyster and let out a gasp as the fork glanced off the shell and landed in the soft squishy park of her other hand—the one holding the shell—between the thumb and forefinger. For a moment there was nothing, then pain snapped and red started to ooze out of her skin.

"Oh my God." Her breathing came in rapid gasps as she pulled the fork back. The cut didn't look big at all, but a thin rivulet of blood ran down her palm. A pulsing sting echoed through her body, embarrassment mixing with the pain.

"Did you just…?" Beckett leaned forward, his eyes widening. "Shit."

He grabbed the linen napkin from his lap and wadded it up, coming around the side of the table to press it against her hand to stem the bleeding. How in the hell did she manage to make herself look like such an idiot? She told the guy to take her on a date, and what did she do? She bloody stabbed herself.

Like a moron.

"Are you okay?" Beckett was suddenly close—too close—his aftershave and the wine on his lips invading her nostrils. The warm touch of his hand holding the napkin over her sending heat flaring through her body.

Oh shit. Oh shit. Oh shit.

People were starting to look at them. A waiter was making his way over, brows creased, as more people turned to look. It was just like that time she knocked over the Baccarat vase at a charity event. She could practically feel the scorn clawing at her skin.

Who the hell buys a five-thousand-dollar vase anyway?

"McKenna?" Beckett frowned. "You're breathing really funny. Are you okay?"

"I'm fine." The words barely came out.

"Miss?" The waiter was suddenly at their table. "Is everything okay."

"I'm *fine*," she repeated.

"We had an incident with the oyster fork," Beckett said.

We. Like they were in it together. God, she could only imagine what Gage would have done. If he hadn't laughed at her, he probably would have left her to deal with it on her own. But Beckett was here, still touching her. Still comforting her with his free hand resting at her back.

"Here, let's have a look," Beckett said.

"Wait—" she protested, but he was already pulling the napkin back and blood rushed from the small wound.

It was so red. So very red.

"Oh no." Her vision swam.

Then it went dark.

McKenna blinked, golden dots flashing in her vision. No, they weren't dots. They were light-fittings. Groaning, she pushed up into a sitting position.

"Careful." Beckett stern tone made her wince, but he eased her up.

"What happened?" Her voice was groggy. Her brain scrambled to try and put the pieces together.

"You were out for a second." His blue eyes searched her face, brows knitted above his perfect nose. "Just long enough for me to carry you out here."

"Where are we?" It looked similar to the restaurant but they were in a small room with an empty table. She appeared to be lying on a couch.

"We're still at Tide Pool. Thankfully their private dining suite wasn't booked tonight." He sat stiffly beside her, looking as though he wanted to say more—or *do* more—but wasn't sure how to proceed. "They're calling an ambulance."

"What? No!" She shook her head. "Oh God, this is so embarrassing. I don't need an ambulance."

The pulsing started up in her hand again. The linen napkin was now mottled with red and pink, but the bleeding appeared to have stopped. She swayed a little and wrenched her eyes away.

"I just…get woozy at the sight of blood." She cringed. "Funny how I could make the grossest flesh-eating monster in my SFX class at makeup school and be totally fine, but at the tiniest drop of real blood…boom. Out like a light."

His lip twitched, and she couldn't tell if it was a smile or something else. "I'm glad I was standing next to you. You went down fast."

Ordinarily that would have been a perfect "that's what she said" opportunity, but McKenna was too mortified to make jokes. "Can you please tell them not to call the ambulance? I'm fine, honestly."

"You sure?" He checked her face, though she wasn't sure what he was looking for since he wasn't a doctor.

"I am. I'll even go to see my mother tomorrow so she can check out my hand, okay? I have her on speed dial if anything happens."

"Okay," he said reluctantly, as he pushed up from the chair. "Do you want to go back in and finish our dinner?"

And walk past all those people who probably thought she was a freak who didn't even know how to use her silverware? No, thank you. She shook her head.

"Don't go anywhere, okay?" he said. "I'll be back."

...

Beckett thanked the Tide Pool manager with a brusque shake of the hand as he settled the bill. Or rather, as he *tried* to settle the bill. The manager insisted that what little food they'd eaten be comped, so that Beckett and McKenna would return for another romantic dinner in the future. Beckett didn't bother to correct the man that there wasn't supposed to be anything romantic about his date with McKenna. In theory, anyway.

She'd seemed more embarrassed than hurt, which was fine by him. Better that her ego be a little bruised than anything be wrong with her physically. The second she'd slumped against him, his heart had leaped into his mouth and he'd rushed to hide her away from those gawking eyes. People were animals when it came to that stuff—couldn't they mind their own business instead of ogling some poor woman who'd fainted?

That moment on the couch—when her eyes had still been closed and her lips parted—something had struck him in the chest. He cared about her, in some way. He was worried for this quirky, sparkly, funny woman who was basically a stranger. Well, maybe not a stranger...but he didn't really *know* her.

Shaking off the weird thoughts, Beckett pushed open the door to the private dining area. McKenna was sitting up, her blue eyes looking more alert than a few moments ago. She also appeared to have cleaned up her hand in the private bathroom there. The napkin was gone, and so was the blood.

"Do we have to amputate?" he asked with a mock serious tone.

She rolled her eyes, but a smile pulled at her lips. "It's touch and go. I'll have to keep an eye on it."

He held out her coat, which he'd collected from the

manager. "How about we get some fresh air?"

She nodded. "Good idea."

She let him help her into the coat, slipping one arm into each sleeve. Against his better judgment, he swept her hair out from the collar. It was silky and thick, the purple ends glistening like magic under the intimate lighting. That was McKenna in a nutshell: magic. Otherworldly.

Like she'd been born in another realm and had been dropped off on Earth by mistake.

He smoothed his hands over her shoulders and she turned, blinking up at him with those big blue eyes, those fringy mink lash things making her look like a doll. A perfect porcelain doll. Something glittered on her eyelids. Black and sparkly like the sky at night. Smudgy. And, God, sexy as anything.

McKenna's breath hitched. "Gee, it's, uh, warm in here."

"Yes." He couldn't seem to say anything else.

"We should go outside now."

He didn't want to. Right then, he wanted nothing more than to lean forward and press his lips to hers. To see if she tasted like sprinkles and cupcake icing. To see if it would be as all-consuming as he suspected.

"After you," he said stiffly, pulling himself away and shrugging into his own coat.

Her heels clicked quick and sharp across the floorboards as she all but ran from the room. *Christ*. What was he doing acting like he wanted something with her? They were here so he could get his ex back. The woman he wanted to marry.

He followed her outside and shoved his hands into his pockets. It was a typical Melbourne winter night—a damp chill on the air, drizzling rain that would relentlessly soak through your coat without you noticing it. The Southbank boulevard gleamed with moisture and a dark river reflected the glittering city lights.

Beckett popped his umbrella. It was one of those small travel-sized ones that folded up small enough to fit into the deep pockets at his hip.

"You really do think of everything, don't you?" McKenna immediately stepped closer to him, sheltering herself. "I bet you were a boy scout."

"Briefly," he replied.

They stood aimlessly at the edge of the river, watching one of the night cruise boats floating along. Most of the guests were inside, save for a brave soul who stood with an umbrella in one hand and a drink in the other.

"Sounds like there's a story there," she said.

"Not really." He smiled at a memory. "I just preferred LAN parties over camping."

"LAN parties. Like those geek meet-ups where you all hooked your computers up and played games overnight." She looked up at him. "Or what was it called when you would take the contents of someone's computer? Leeching?"

Beckett raised a brow. Now *that* was not something he expected her to know. "Are you a secret nerd, McKenna?"

"Uh, no. But my brother Jason used to go to them all the time. I think that's how he used to get his porn." She wrinkled her nose. "He hosted a small one years back while my parents were at some gala dinner. I snuck down to see what they were doing…"

"And?"

"I saw a lot of boobs and things getting blown up. Can't say I was too keen to ever get involved after that."

Beckett nodded. "Ours were mostly friends playing multiplayer first-person shooters like Counter-Strike. Highly nerdy and unattractive, I can assure you."

She grinned. "Oh, I don't know about that. Hand-eye coordination is a valuable skill to have."

Something about the way she said it made him think she

wasn't referring to video games. McKenna's cheeks were flushed pink and she gave a little shiver next to him.

"You're cold," he said, frowning.

She raised a brow. "You asking or telling?"

"You're shivering."

"Ah, telling. Got it." Her tongue darted out to moisten her lips. "This is going to sound terrible since I just abandoned our dinner but…"

"You're hungry."

"Getting real good at anticipating my feelings, aren't you?" She rubbed her hands up and down her arms. "I'm sorry I ruined the fancy dinner."

"It's okay. It was only a fake date, anyway." He bumped her with his elbow. "Come on. This way."

Chapter Eight

Fifteen minutes later, Beckett and McKenna were seated on a hard-plastic Crayola yellow bench. They were separated from the deteriorating weather by a plastic tarp, which covered the "outdoor" dining area. Rain pelted steadily against the plastic. It could have been a dreary turn of events, if it wasn't for the glorious twinkle in McKenna's eye as she held a McChicken burger so reverently that it may as well have been a Michelin-starred masterpiece.

"McChickens are *vastly* superior to Big Macs," she said, gesturing with a fry. "What the hell is secret sauce, anyway? I don't want secrets in my food."

"One, it's 'special' sauce. Not secret sauce. And two, you're eating highly processed chicken from a fast food restaurant." Beckett took a bite out of his Big Mac. "There's a whole lot of secrecy going on there."

"Nuh-uh." She flipped the lid on her burger and stuffed a few fries in, trapping them between the bun and the chicken. "God, I'm so hungry I could eat three of these."

She chewed happily, a dot of sauce on her cheek that

made Beckett want to grin from ear to ear for some stupid reason. "Trust me. I ate a lot of burgers in my formative years in university."

"Your *formative* years?" She rolled her eyes.

"McDonalds is standard coding food," he said. "Fact."

"So you subsisted on a steady diet of Big Macs, cheap beer, and Twisties?"

"Cheezels," he corrected. "But yeah, essentially."

Her eyes raked over him, a skeptical quirk on her lips. "I somehow doubt you ended up with that body by eating junk." A second later, her brain seemed to have caught up with her mouth and she grimaced. "What I mean is that you look too fit…uh, muscular." She swore under her breath. "Well, I *have* seen you topless so I know you're not skinny fat."

He tried to stifle his smile. "Dig up."

"Oh, be quiet," she grumbled and took another bite of her burger. "You've got a great body. It's a fact. I'm not telling you anything you don't already know."

Beckett wasn't a gym junkie by any means, but he always seemed to have energy to burn. Going for a run was the best way to clear his head when the code wouldn't cooperate—so he was fit. Muscular. That *was* a fact. But hearing her say it stoked some primal, egotistical part of him.

A part that usually only flared around work-related things.

"Okay, change of topic," she announced. "Tell me about your sister. What do I need to know to make sure I nail my meeting with her?"

"You're the makeup artist." He shrugged. "How do I tell you about that?"

"Tell me about *her*. What's she like? How does she dress?" She brought her drink up to her lips and sucked, leaving a perfect pink line on the straw. "That kind of stuff."

"Kayla is very…" He thought for a moment. "She likes

fashion. She's outgoing."

"Okay." McKenna rolled her hand around. "Keep going."

What else was he supposed to say about his little sister? He knew all the things that wouldn't matter to a makeup artist—like that she was still terrified her husband-to-be would leave her just like her father did. That she was whip-smart, witty. Emotionally intelligent. Great with people. Basically, his opposite.

"She's classic," he said after a pause. "She likes Audrey Hepburn movies."

"Okay, now we're getting somewhere." He could see McKenna's mind drifting. "I'm thinking winged liner, nothing too dramatic but a nice little flick. Some feathered false lashes, maybe. Or individual clusters. Fresh skin."

Wasn't all skin fresh? And what the hell were individual clusters?

"Why did you decide to become a makeup artist?" he asked.

"I've always liked makeup," she replied. "I used to sit and watch my mum get ready for all these big events when I was little. I love the transformation. Makeup can turn you into anyone."

Her eyes were alight with passion; it radiated from her like a wave of energy. It was exactly how he felt when he was talking about his business.

"I used to experiment a lot when I was younger, and all my friends would get me to do their makeup. It makes me feel like a fairy godmother." She popped a fry into her mouth. "That moment when you hold a mirror up to the client's face and see their confidence blossom is truly a wonderful thing."

"And they always like the makeup?"

"Yeah, mostly. But I've had a few disasters in my career, too. They happen." She chuckled. "One time, this woman brought her daughter to the counter for a special event. The mother stood over me the whole time, telling me that *this* bit wasn't even and *that* bit wasn't blended properly."

"What did you do?"

"I handed her my makeup brush and told her that if she thought she could do a better job then she was welcome to finish it." She nodded, pride etched into her features. "I thought the floor manager was going to kill me, but it worked. The daughter ended up loving the makeup and the mother didn't make a complaint. I'm sure you have to deal with difficult people in your line of work, right?"

"It's a different dynamic."

"Because you work for yourself?"

He nodded. "And because it can take a while to create the product."

"Does it feel like you're in that grind for months and months? Must be, since you work such long hours." She studied him. "How do you think you're going to fix things with Sherri if your work isn't going to change?"

Her question struck him in the chest. Of course his work wasn't going to change, but that didn't mean he couldn't smooth things over with Sherri. She needed to see that he still loved her, that was all.

So why did he suddenly feel like a weight had settled on his chest? That caged feeling was back—the one that made his heart and lungs want to cave under the pressure of walls closing in.

"I have to fix it," he said. "That's why I need you."

"You mean, need my *help*," she corrected him.

He swallowed. "Right. Exactly."

• • •

By the time Monday rolled around, McKenna was a bundle of nerves. Beckett's sister, Kayla, had called over the weekend to set a time for their catch up. Instead of having a meeting, Kayla wanted to jump right into doing a trial. Turns out she hadn't found a makeup artist she liked after four trials. *Four.*

What makes you think you're going to be any better than any of these other artists? They probably have more experience than you, and a better portfolio. And I bet their families support them, too.

God, her inner voice was such a bitch sometimes.

McKenna sucked in a breath and jabbed at the doorbell to the stunning white townhouse. A tune played inside, something that caused a memory to spark. It was a classical piece. A failed ballet exam.

"Don't panic," she told herself. "Be cool, calm, and collected. You're a cucumber. A talented, professional cucumber."

A second later the door swung open and a gorgeous pixie of a woman stood in front of her. "You must be McKenna. Come in."

"Lovely to meet you," McKenna replied as she stepped into the house, rolling her kit in behind her. She'd fashioned a carry-on suitcase into her perfect travel kit, which made it a hell of a lot easier than lugging a case around. "You have a beautiful home."

Kayla beamed. She had Beckett's blue eyes but her hair was darker—more chestnut brown than his sandy dark blond. She also smiled more readily than he did—but the smile was similar. Slightly crooked. Charmingly off-center.

"Thank you." She motioned for McKenna to follow her into the main area of the house. "Will we be okay to do the trial in here? I figured you'd need natural light and this room has the most at this time of day."

"It's perfect."

"So, my brother was a little quiet on how you two know each other," Kayla said, interest twinkling in her eyes. "Tea?"

"Yes, please." McKenna stopped next to the dining table and dropped down to open her kit. "I live a few doors down from him."

"He's never mentioned you before." The question wasn't accusing, more curious.

"Well, we don't really know each other that well. But when he mentioned you were getting married I sort of took the opportunity to pimp my business." She laughed. "Honesty's the best policy, right?"

"Absolutely." The kettle whistled and Kayla poured the boiling water into two cups.

McKenna pulled out her brush roll and opened it up, and started to unpack the products she would need for skin prep. During their quick phone call over the weekend, McKenna had gotten necessary information—skin type, skin concerns, and a rough idea of the look that Kayla wanted for her big day. Audrey Hepburn old-school glam, with a touch of J-Lo. It was a unique description, that was for sure.

"So tell me about what disappointed you with the previous makeup trials," McKenna said. "It's not for gossip, but to give me a better idea of what you *don't* want. That's as important to know as what you *do* want."

"Gosh, four trials and I'm still not happy," Kayla said sheepishly. She set the tea down on the table and slid onto the fold-out stool McKenna had pulled out of her kit. "That must make me sound like such a bridezilla."

"Not at all. Finding the right makeup artist is a very personal thing." She looked closely at Kayla's skin—it was flawless, which would make her job easier.

"Well, I suspect the first artist wasn't as qualified as she claimed to be." Kayla watched as McKenna massaged some anti-bacterial gel into her hands. "She was a friend of a friend, and the makeup wasn't much better than what I could do myself."

"Ah, I see." She scooped some hydrating cream out of a pot with a tiny spatula and then proceeded to prep Kayla's skin.

"The second trial was great, actually. I was going to book her, but she had a family emergency and then had to move back to Singapore suddenly." Kayla sighed. "The other two… well, the makeup wasn't what I'd envisaged for my wedding. It's such a special day, and I want to get every detail right. One lady put *way* too much bronzer on me and she seemed keen on making me look as tanned as possible. The other one struggled with the winged liner I wanted, and kept trying to talk me out of it."

"Got it. Winged liner, not too much bronzer." She grinned. "It's good that you know exactly what you want. It's harder for me when the bride has no idea, then it becomes a bit of a crapshoot as to whether they'll like the end product."

"If there's one thing people in our family *don't* have an issue with, it's knowing what we want." Kayla chuckled. "I guess Beckett and I get that from our mother. She's stubborn as hell, and so are we."

McKenna pumped some primer onto her palette and used a soft brush to sweep it over Kayla's skin, adding a dewy "lit from within" glow. "Better than drifting through life with no idea of what you want, I think."

"Try telling Beckett's fiancée that." Kayla rolled her eyes. "She's determined to get him to change everything he wants to what *she* wants."

Was Beckett's sister unaware of the breakup? Interesting.

"Don't get me wrong, she's a nice person. I know she doesn't mean to treat him like crap, but they're wrong for each other and it causes a lot of friction."

McKenna bit down on her lip and concentrated on testing foundation shades against her client's jawline. What was she supposed to do? She didn't want to spill the beans if Beckett had chosen to keep the breakup a secret, but she didn't want to seem disinterested, either.

"How long have they been together?" she asked carefully. Using her thumb and forefinger, she gently gripped Kayla's jaw and moved her head to check the foundation swatches from a different angle. Yep, option two was a perfect match.

"They've been engaged for almost a year and they were together for a year before that," Kayla said. "But they've broken up a few times, here and there. He'll do something that pisses her off, she'll have a tantrum, and then they split up for a week. I don't know why he doesn't send her packing for good. Probably because her father is so heavily invested in his business."

McKenna frowned, but covered it quickly by pretending to intently study Kayla's skin as she applied the foundation with a synthetic brush. "Oh?"

"Yeah, her dad is some huge bigwig. He was the main backer for Beckett's latest project, so he probably feels stuck because if they break up then that money will likely go away." She sighed. "I tried to tell him that my fiancé's family might be able to invest, but he's got this thing about making sure I'm not tied to Aaron for money's sake. Which is kind of ridiculous, considering."

A strange feeling churned in McKenna's gut. Beckett had seemed so caring on their test date—gruffly caring... but caring none the less. The guy who'd tended to her injury, who'd walked away from a fancy restaurant to have dinner at McDonalds because she was too scared to go back, who'd dropped her off at her front door with a smoldering look and a respectful peck on the cheek...he didn't seem like a guy who would be in a relationship for money's sake.

"It's sad. He deserves someone who'll make him laugh," Kayla added. "I think Sherri stresses him out. She doesn't seem to take much interest in his work. Or his family, for that matter."

"It sounds like you guys are close," McKenna said, desperate to steer the conversation away from his ex.

"Yeah, he was my rock growing up. Now I have Aaron, of course." Her eyes became dreamy and soft.

McKenna inspected Kayla's jawline to make sure the foundation had blended properly, without leaving a harsh edge. "How did you two meet? Tell me all about it."

McKenna breathed an internal sigh of relief as Kayla switched gears and started talking about her fiancé.

It had been all too easy to feel like her date with Beckett—post oyster fork incident—was real. They'd connected on some personal level, laughed and joked and chatted for hours over burgers and then sundaes. On the way home, McKenna wondered why she couldn't have found Beckett before. They had a lot in common, they seemed to like the same things. And the chemistry fizzed and crackled like nothing else.

But that was just McKenna doing what she always did: gravitating to the wrong guy.

Which meant Operation Self-Love had to be priority number one. And if Beckett was the kind of guy who wanted to marry for money, then he wasn't the guy for her anyway.

Chapter Nine

"You know you don't have to fix every little thing when you come over." Beckett's mother, Minnie, stood with her arms folded across her chest. Her hair was sticking out in every direction, failing to be tamed by the red bandanna tied around her head. "I'm perfectly capable of changing light bulbs and dusting cobwebs."

"Kayla makes dinner and I fix stuff." Beckett grunted as he fiddled with the bulb in his mother's old-fashioned—and fussy as hell—light fixture. "That's how it works."

It could have sounded chauvinistic. Or, at the very least, pointlessly upholding gender stereotypes that he was fixing and his sister was cooking. But, on offering to assist with dinner, Kayla had shooed him out of the kitchen under the threat of bodily harm with a rubber mallet.

"Two bloody peas in a pod," his mother muttered.

"Sorry Aaron couldn't make it tonight," Kayla said as she pounded away at the chicken breasts, winking at Beckett when their mother wasn't looking. "He's working such long hours lately. I feel like I hardly see him."

"Does that bother you?" Beckett asked as he finally got the bulb to pop into place. After dealing with a complex coding issue today, requiring several hours sitting in the same position, his muscles protested being stretched.

"That he works a lot?" Kayla looked up. "Sometimes. But I get it, he's in that stage of his career where he needs to prove himself. I'm sure a time will come where I'm working long hours and he'll be wishing I was home."

Beckett shook his head. "See, it's not unreasonable," he muttered to himself.

Certainly not the catastrophic event that Sherri had made it out to be. Make hay while the sun shines, that was his motto. Hard work now would afford them the luxury to take life at a slower pace later on. One didn't get the reward without first getting their hands dirty.

Besides, he *liked* his job. He thrived on the stress and the deadlines and the problem solving. It made him feel alive. And that was a hell of a lot more than what most people could say.

"Sherri giving you a hard time about it again?" Kayla asked. "She doesn't understand how passionate you are about your work."

Minnie rolled her eyes. "Probably because she never had to work for anything herself."

"Don't say that," Beckett said. "She works hard and she got that job on her own merits."

Beckett shot them both a look as he climbed down the stepladder. *This* was exactly why he hadn't told them about the latest breakup. Lord knew he didn't need the extra drama from his family when they inevitably got back together.

Not that Sherri would afford him the same courtesy. God only knew what she'd said to her father this time—that he was some greedy bastard who ignored her and was married to his work.

Beckett frowned. Okay, maybe that wasn't entirely off base…except for the greedy bit. It wasn't that he intentionally ignored her, but some days he got so far into the zone that he tuned the rest of the world out. He'd always been like that—so focused and intent on achieving his goals that he lost himself in his work, in the lines of code and the cloud of ideas that fogged up his brain.

Then why have you been thinking about McKenna all day?

He shrugged off the little voice in his head that seemed intent on taunting him.

"Oh, Beckett. I meant to tell you that I had my makeup trial with your friend on Monday," Kayla said. "She's so lovely. And *gorgeous.* I thought you were just yanking my chain with that whole thing about her being attractive. Why didn't you tell me you were serious?"

"I didn't think her appearance would matter for applying makeup," he said drily.

"But no denial that's she pretty…interesting." Kayla grinned.

Oh boy. *This* was why he wasn't keen on McKenna meeting his sister. He knew Kayla would jump on the chance to play matchmaker…never mind the fact that she didn't even know he was single at this stage.

You're temporarily *single and trying to fix it. Don't get attached to the label.*

"Did you like the makeup?" he asked as he came into the kitchen to toss the burned-out bulb.

"I did. I've got one more trial lined up, though." She looked a little sheepish. "I swear I'm not trying to be a bridezilla, but I want everything to be perfect."

"Isn't that the definition of a bridezilla?" their mother teased. "It's only makeup."

"It's important." Kayla frowned. "I know it might seem

silly, but his family is a big deal and there will be a lot of photos…"

Beckett noticed the slight tick in his mother's expression, and the hardening of her mouth. Of course she was supportive of Kayla's choices about the marriage, but there had been an undercurrent of tension brewing for a few weeks now. And it wasn't the first time Kayla had called her fiancé's family "a big deal."

"I'm sure McKenna would do a great job," he said, trying to steer the conversation back toward the fluffier side before things got too tense. "Her makeup always looks nice."

"Since when do *you* notice someone's makeup?" Kayla laughed. "I still remember the time Sherri came home with a new lipstick and flipped out because you said you couldn't tell the difference. Granted, it takes a certain level of perception to tell the difference between two types of beige…"

"I figure it's more relevant for me to notice McKenna's makeup, since she's a makeup artist. After all, I *did* pass on her details to you." He rolled his eyes. "How could I recommend someone without first assessing their skill level?"

Kayla looked intently down at the dinner she was preparing, trying to disguise her smirk by focusing on cracking an egg into a bowl. "Just how much assessment have you done?"

"Don't wind him up," Minnie said, shooting a conspiratorial look at Kayla. "You know he takes things seriously."

"One of us has to," he muttered.

"Hey!" Kayla and Minnie said at the same time.

His sister narrowed her eyes at him. "I take things seriously, but I also don't live my life like every decision is life or death."

Beckett scoffed. "Taking responsibility for my work and my finances is not living like everything is life or death. It's called being an adult."

Minnie shook her head. "You are too much like your father, Beck. You'll dig yourself an early grave with all that stress."

"Someone has to take care of you."

Shit. He wasn't planning on having this discussion tonight, but it looked like his worries had been bubbling away more than he'd thought. Not to mention Kayla's comment about him enabling her—that had been eating away at him, too.

"I never asked for your goddamn money," his mother said, her blue eyes blazing. "I'm perfectly capable of looking after myself. Did it from the day you were in diapers and I can do it now."

"Really?" He folded his arms across his chest. "And how are you going to do that without a job?"

"You told him?" Minnie shot daggers at Kayla, who sighed.

"Yes, Ma. I told him." She shook her head as she proceeded to dip the flattened chicken breasts into a bowl of flour and then egg. "I was worried."

"I can do without the judgment, thank you very much. From both of you." His mother folded her arms across her chest, her features settled into a dark expression. "I refuse to work in an environment where I'm not treated properly. And that manager is an idiot. I can't work for idiots."

Beckett looked skyward, digging as deep as he could to find the willpower not to remind his mother of all the other jobs she'd quit for similarly tenuous reasons. His mother's issue with authority was more the catalyst for her employment flakiness than any of her managers' lack of capability. Or her being treated poorly. In fact, at her last job, he had met the manager and had thought very highly of him. But Minnie Walsh did *not* like being told what to do. That was the bottom line.

"Besides," Minnie said with a falsely nonchalant tone. "Greg's moving back in. So I'll have someone to help out with the bills."

"*What*?" Beckett and Kayla both exclaimed at the same time.

Greg was Kayla's father and possibly the only person in the world who made Minnie look like a pillar of employment stability. He'd relied on his family's money for years, but Beckett had his suspicions that they'd cut him off a few years back. Not that they'd seen the man in at least half a decade—had no idea where he'd been, if he was dead or alive. It wasn't like he called Kayla on her birthday or even sent a card.

"Has he been back here already?" Kayla's hurt expression made anger wrench in Beckett's chest. "I haven't heard from him."

"Oh, he's been in and out." Minnie looked oblivious to her daughter's pain.

"Sounds like him." Beckett's jaw clenched. "He waltzes in and out as he pleases, with no regard for taking care of his family."

"He's a free soul, you know that. And I'd rather him be like that than tie himself to me for the wrong reasons." His mother shot him a meaningful look.

Beckett rolled his eyes at the thinly veiled commentary on his relationship with Sherri. "Oh, and wanting to build a stable and secure life with someone is the wrong reason?"

"You should be more concerned with finding someone you love. Someone who excites you." Minnie threw her hands up in the air. "Not someone who spends her every waking moment trying to guilt you into changing."

Did Sherri excite him? No. But why was excitement a measure of a good relationship? It was far down on Beckett's list of needs. And, from what he'd seen, Minnie's definition of excitement meant being with a man so selfish he'd disappear without a word for years at a time. Why the hell would anyone want that?

"At least when he's here I know it's because he wants to be here, not because he feels obligated," Minnie added.

"And what about what his daughter wants, huh?" Beckett shook his head. "Did that occur to either of you?"

"Stop it!" Kayla slapped her hand down on the kitchen counter. "Beck, I appreciate the support but I can speak for myself. And Ma, just…tell Dad I *would* like to hear from him. I don't think that's too much to ask."

Beckett dug his fingers into the back of his neck, kneading the tight muscles there. Kayla was right, she could speak for herself. But it killed him to see the way his mother was so oblivious to how Greg's actions affected her daughter. It'd been this way for over twenty years, and nothing had changed. Greg would come and go without warning, Minnie would always welcome him back, and they both would forget about Kayla's feelings.

Not exactly a great example of a successful relationship. It was hard not to wonder how their lives may have turned out if his father had beaten the cancer that took him so young. But then he wouldn't have Kayla for a sister, and Beckett wouldn't give her up for anything. Which made those lines of thinking pointless.

And sure, what he had with Sherri wasn't for everyone, but it worked for him.

Did it, really?

A little voice of disquiet needled at him, but Beckett shut the thought down. Of *course* it worked. Sure, Sherri could be demanding and he could be distant, and their communication styles didn't exactly mesh. But they'd had a lot of good times together over the years. He was doing the right thing. Being with Sherri was what he wanted—they would work out the kinks in their differences in expectation. Eventually.

But why then did McKenna suddenly pop into his head, unbidden.

You have a plan and you're going to stick to it. No detours. No distractions.

. . .

McKenna walked along the street to her apartment building, her chin buried in a thick wooly scarf. It was dark and drizzly outside. Miserable, like her. She hurried along the pavement, cursing herself for wearing heels when flats would have been far easier and more comfortable. But she'd developed this habit of dressing outrageously for family dinners—a little middle finger action to her parents' overly conservative views on personal appearance.

And really, pink glitter stilettos were the *only* thing that would go with a silver sequined dress.

She laughed bitterly. Her mother had looked like her head was about to explode when McKenna had walked into their foyer. Her brother, Jason, had stifled a snort behind his hand, but his girlfriend had looked horrified. And McKenna wasn't even showing *that* much cleavage. Truth was, she hated the dress—it was too tight and felt scratchy against her skin. But she hated being forced into a box even more.

She walked through the front doors of the apartment building and gave a wave to the concierge. The heating was cranked to accommodate for the unusually shitty weather—even by Melbourne's standards—but she didn't want to take her coat off yet. She'd wait for the safety of the elevator.

"Yeah, because it's fine to give your family an eyeful but you wouldn't want to flash the concierge," she muttered as she jabbed the up button.

When the doors slid open, she stepped inside without checking the direction and found herself heading down instead of up. Sighing, she hit the button for her floor and shucked her coat. A second later, once they'd hit the basement parking area, the doors slid open.

Beckett stood there, wearing well-fitting jeans and a navy V-neck jumper that clung to the muscles in his chest. His stormy expression dissolved when he saw her—his brows lifting out of a frown like sunshine breaking through clouds. Dammit, how did he do that?

His gaze raked her over as he stepped into the elevator and stood beside her. "Coming or going?"

She stifled the urge to play with the double-entendre, not wanting to discourage him from talking to her instead of grunting like he used to. "Coming."

"It's early."

"Not early enough," she said with a wry grin. "It was a family dinner."

"Oh." He raised a brow, looking a little confused. She couldn't blame him—it looked like she'd gone shopping in the sale section of Club Rats R US. "I had one of those, too."

His tone said that his night had been about as good as hers. "Why are families so difficult?"

He laughed. The deep, smooth sound rippled through the air, sending a pulse of awareness through her. She almost sighed at the little shiver that darted down her spine. Was it possible for her ears to have an orgasm? Because she was pretty sure they just had.

"I don't know." He shook his head.

"It's like they try to be difficult, you know?" She mimicked his action. "I mean, I've resorted to dressing like this"—she waved a hand up and down in front of her—"to distract them from talking about the *real* ways I disappoint them. I'm basically Vegas Bender Barbie at this point. And for what? So they'll talk about my skanky outfit instead of telling me, yet again, that I should consider going to university so I can get a real job?"

The silence that followed her outburst was broken only by the cheerful *ping* of the elevator. Wow, that had gotten a little too real a little too quickly.

"I'm sure you have no idea what that's like," she said, hoping to hell her face wasn't as shiny and pink as her shoes. "I mean, you're a big, successful entrepreneur and all. Your family must be really proud of you."

They stepped into the hallway and Beckett looked at her, his intense blue gaze drilling right through the sparkle and flesh until it hit bone. "Do you want ice cream?"

McKenna blinked. "Huh?"

"I have some in my freezer." He cocked his head.

It was impossible to read a man like Beckett. But she figured the offer of food was a good thing. Had she somehow broken through that tough outer shell? The thought warmed her far more than it should have.

"Sure." She couldn't stop a smile spreading over her lips. "But I'll get changed first, if that's okay. This dress sheds like crazy and I don't want to defile your couch."

Oh God. *Wrong. Choice. Of. Word.*

Defiling Beckett's couch—*with* Beckett—was exactly what she wanted right now. She had all this pent-up energy and he looked tastier than a giant slab of cheesecake. Luckily for her, he seemed to take her intended, rather than Freudian, meaning.

"Sure. I'll leave the door unlocked." His eyes skated over her one more time, leaving fire blazing in her blood, before he headed toward his apartment.

Biting down on her lip to stifle another stupid, dangerous smile, McKenna unlocked her front door.

She was going to hang out with Beckett. A simple dessert between family dinner survivors wouldn't be so bad, would it?

"It is," she scolded herself. "Because you want to jump his bones."

So true. She *did* want to jump his bones. Even Mr. Whopper was getting jealous. But that would be bad for the plan. Bad for Operation Self-Love.

Her breath hitched. What if he'd stripped and was taking a shower? It was all too easy to imagine the hard muscle beneath his sensible button-down shirts. He was the hot IT nerd of her dreams.

She pulled up Emery's number and shook her head as she typed.

McKenna: Help!!! I'm having a self-love emergency.

Emery: You know I love you…but not like that.

McKenna smirked. Trust Emery's mind to go straight to the gutter.

McKenna: Not that kind of self-love emergency. There's a guy…there's not supposed to be a guy!

Emery: Sexy toy guy?

McKenna: Can we not call him that?

Emery: STG for short.

McKenna: Fine. He's too tempting. I'm about to have ice cream at his place. Having visions of defiling his couch. How did this happen???

Emery: Are you planning to check something off the sex bucket list??

Emery then sent a string of eggplant emojis, and McKenna shook her head.

McKenna: You're supposed to be my self-love Sherpa.

Emery: I never agreed to that.

McKenna: What should I do??

Emery: …

The three little dots in the bottom corner of her phone's screen taunted her. Emery never gave that much thought to a text—it was straight from her brain to her fingers. No filter.

McKenna: Well?

Emery: Is he the right guy?

McKenna put the phone down and huffed. The whole reason she even imposed Operation Self-Love was because of her inability to pick the right men. That was, men who didn't think she was vapid or stupid for her career choice, who wouldn't put pressure on her to change. Who didn't think she talked too much. And that went double for guys who'd just gotten dumped by the person they were supposed to marry.

She'd been the rebound girl before. Not. Fun.

McKenna: No, he's not the right guy. He's totally Mr. Wrong.

Emery: Then pick up a vibrator and move on.

Emery was right. What the hell was McKenna doing with her life? Wasn't the very definition of insanity making the same mistake over and over while hoping for a different result? But before McKenna had the chance to figure out what to do about Beckett, her phone started to vibrate.

"Crap," McKenna muttered. Her mother's number flashed up on the screen.

She *never* called to chat. If there was one thing McKenna had worked out about her mother—it was that a phone call meant she was about to get bitched out.

"Hello?" She tried to sound like she'd picked up the phone in a rush, without seeing who'd called.

"McKenna." Her mother was the only person who could instill such gut-twisting emotion with only the use of her name. "I was going to let it go tonight, I really was…"

"What were you going to let go?" She tried to keep the exasperation out of her voice, because there was nothing that fired Amy Prescott up faster than the sound of someone sighing.

"Your dress, your attitude…just you!"

"Oh, so the usual then?" She cringed as soon as the words flew out of her mouth. How was it that the second she had to deal with her family she regressed to this sarcasm-loaded way of communicating? It was like their mere presence turned her into a sulky teenager.

But dammit, she was so sick of them and their judgmental attitudes.

"You cannot turn up to a family dinner dressed like you're about to go work a street corner."

McKenna looked at herself in the mirror of her bedroom. The silver sequined dress had thin little straps that followed the curve of her shoulders and a built-in bustier which pushed her boobs up. She'd worn a black cardigan over the top, because it was cold out, but it didn't do much to dull the impact of the dress. Sure, it was a little over the top for dinner. And sure, she'd worn it to prove a point.

But having her mother tell her she looked like a hooker… well, that was low. Even for Amy.

"I have to afford my crack habit somehow," she said sarcastically. "Also, it's usually dark out and sequins reflect the car's headlights. So really, it's a safety thing."

"McKenna, you are just…" Her mother broke off in an irritated huff. "I try so hard with you but you refuse to listen to anyone. Your life could be so great, you could have the world at your feet. But you make stupid decision after stupid decision."

The pause stretched out for several heartbeats and McKenna could practically see her mother shaking her head.

"You can't expect anyone to support you if you continue to act like a child," she added. "I can't say I'm surprised that Gage wouldn't put up with it."

McKenna swallowed, anger burning a path up the back of her throat. "What's the real problem? That I came to dinner with my boobs out or that I refuse to let you stifle me with your life plans."

"Stifle you? I'm trying to *enlighten* you. I'm trying to help you see that you need to change."

Amy was right. McKenna *did* need to change. She needed to take charge of her life and go after the things that she wanted. She needed to change by not being afraid of failure. And, most importantly, she needed to change by seeing that her family might never support her dreams…and she needed to be okay with that.

"I appreciate your concern," McKenna said. "But I'm not going to be your Mini Me. Sorry, but that's not the life I want."

Chapter Ten

After hanging up on her mother and then ditching the sequined monstrosity, McKenna changed outfits three times in under two minutes. Going to Beckett's might not be the smartest move, but dammit she was riled up right now. Listening to her parents' lectures always drove her in the opposite direction to what they'd intended. Why should she feel guilty for being who she was?

And that comment about Gage…

Oh, it made her see red. She hastily wiped off her hot-pink lipstick and replaced it with a tinted lip balm, then wound her purple hair into a fat bun on top of her head. Nothing could be done about the heavy eye makeup without taking the whole thing off and starting again. So the smudgy black shadow and false lashes would have to stay.

"Why do you even care?" She rolled her eyes as she shut the door on her apartment and headed to Beckett's place. "You know they'll never come around."

She glanced at the numbers on Beckett's door and swallowed. Right now, she had bigger problems to deal with, namely the fact that her body started humming at the thought of seeing him again.

Shit. That *wasn't* supposed to happen.

"You're a big girl. You can totally restrain yourself."

Ugh. Why couldn't he be awkward and dowdy and on the *un*appealing side of the introvert spectrum? And why the hell did a guy like him even need to be chasing an ex-girlfriend?

Ex fiancée, remember? He was going to marry this woman and he wants her back. That means he's not interested in you.

Thinking about Sherri was like having a bucket of ice water tipped all over her. McKenna couldn't help the little ball of resentment unfurling in her stomach. What the hell was so special about Sherri, anyway? What did she have that McKenna didn't?

Oh yeah. McKenna knew *exactly* what Sherri had—family money. And that wasn't something McKenna would ever allow to be a factor in her love life.

She glanced down the hallway back to her apartment. Maybe she should stay in and forget about sexy Beckett and his frozen desserts. But he *had* mentioned a family dinner. Which meant he'd seen his sister. Maybe he'd have the inside info on whether or not she was going to get the wedding gig.

Sucking in a breath, she knocked and then pushed on his front door. "Hello?"

"In the kitchen," he called out.

She found him retrieving a small tub from his freezer. Unlike her, he hadn't changed out of his original clothes. Except for his feet—where a pair of leather boots had been a moment ago he now wore socks. They were bright yellow and had cacti all over them.

"I like your socks," she said, leaning against his kitchen counter.

"They're obnoxious." He popped the lid on the ice cream. "But Kayla bought them for me and she made me promise I'd wear them to dinner."

"Did she choose them because she thinks you're prickly?"

He looked up and shot her a perplexed expression. "You two are scary similar."

"Well, for what it's worth, I don't think you're prickly."

He dug an ice cream scoop into the creamy dessert, which looked to be vanilla with some kind of chocolate and caramel swirls. "What do you think I am, then?"

Hmm. How to handle this question without being too honest? "Umm…"

"Is this the first time you've ever been speechless?" A crooked grin lit up his face. "Should I get in touch with the people who do the *Guinness Book of World Records*?"

"Oh, so now you're chatty." She rolled her eyes. "Funny, I didn't know you were such a joker."

"I'm not, usually." He handed her a bowl of ice cream with two generous scoops.

"So…" She followed him out of the kitchen and into the lounge area of his apartment. When he dropped down onto the couch, she took a spot at the other end, wriggling back into the corner to remind herself to keep her distance. "I don't suppose you got the inside scoop about how I did at the trial?"

"Kayla said she was impressed."

"And?"

"She has one more trial."

"Oh." She tried not to be disappointed. But it wasn't easy, considering her parents had gotten particularly stuck into her earlier that evening. Even the sequined dress hadn't been able to distract them. She wasn't sure which parent was worse—her mother, who constantly told her that working in retail was only acceptable if you were studying for a future career. Or her father, who'd interrupted her so many times she'd started to wonder if maybe she was in some kind of

Sixth Sense situation.

When she'd tried to tell them about her business, not one of them engaged. As far as the Prescotts were concerned, the arts were for people who didn't take life seriously. And, given her website wasn't garnering many hits, let alone conversions, she needed to land this makeup job.

"I told her I thought you were very good," Beckett said.

"You did?" She smiled in spite of her down mood. "Was that because of my 'fringy things'?"

"Yes. And your sparkly things." He pointed to her eyes. "I notice them."

Tears pricked at the backs of her eyes and she blinked them away—horrified that his simple comment might cause her to break down. How was it that this man, whom she barely knew and who'd only made noises at her in the beginning, was more supportive than her own family?

He's getting something out of it. You're helping him get his ex back.

Well, she was supposed to be doing that. "Thanks," she said, looking down into her bowl.

"Do you like the ice cream? I try not to eat a lot of crap, but this is my weakness." He nudged her with his cactus sock-covered foot. "Don't tell anyone, okay?"

McKenna drew a cross on her heart with one finger. "I promise."

"Oh, I almost forgot." Beckett put his ice cream down and reached for a laptop sitting on the coffee table. "I made something for you."

A tiny little seed of warmth unfurled in her chest. "You did?"

He tapped at the keyboard, his long fingers flying. "Yeah, I had a look at your website when you gave me the card for Kayla. And it's not very well designed."

"That's probably because I cobbled it together myself."

She spooned a mouthful of ice cream between her lips. "I work magic on faces, not on screens."

Beckett didn't reply, but a second later the page loaded and McKenna gasped. Instead of her old, basic website with the black banner and a stock image of a few makeup brushes with the pink font that she never could seem to get 100 percent clear, her name jumped out in a pretty, silver font.

The background was black with small purple dots. Edgy, yet still girlie. Exactly like her business cards. A large image on the front showed one of McKenna's first brides—a friend of a friend who'd kindly given her a chance last year. Then it changed to another photo, this time of McKenna herself with her eyes cast down, revealing a subtle smoky eye in shades of mauve and soft pink.

"You made this for me?" she asked in disbelief.

Beckett nodded. He wasn't quite smiling, but his eyes were soft and she now knew that meant he was happy. "Your old site didn't have the best navigation and the design wasn't mobile friendly. This one will adjust the size according to the device. I also built in a private section for your clients to log in where they can fill in a form with all the information you need to do their makeup trial. I probably didn't get all the fields right, but I can help you update them."

McKenna's mouth hung open. She'd looked into getting a professional site made up before, so she knew that to hire someone to do this would have cost her a few thousand dollars. Given the business cards had almost blown her budget, fees for a web designer weren't something she could even consider right now.

"Even if Kayla doesn't hire you, I *know* you'll find more work," he said. "And all businesses need a proper website."

"Thank you." For once she didn't have anything else to say. Emotion clogged the back of her throat. It was such a sweet gesture and, like Beckett, so practical. So thoughtful.

To her complete horror, McKenna burst into tears. The whole day had been a shambles—crappy, rude customers at work followed by dinner with her crappy, rude family. Gage had come by the CAM-Ready Cosmetics counter with his new girlfriend to treat her to some makeup. Ugh, it was like he was showing off a prize poodle. Fucking gag.

And the one person who really had no reason to be kind to her was Beckett. And here he was, feeding her ice cream, building her a website, and being adorably sweet. Gah! Why did he have to be attached to someone else?

"I'm sorry, I just..." She hiccupped. "It's been a long day. My parents think I'm a failure and my brother's snotty girlfriend made a crack about my dress and I'm scared I'm going to be stuck working at the department store forever and everyone thinks I'm stupid. I'm *not* stupid."

Seriously, where was a muzzle when she needed it? But the words continued to flow out of her in some attempt at cathartic release.

"I hate that they're all trying to fit me into this box that isn't me. Why can't they just accept me as I am?" Her face felt as though it was burning from the inside out. Beckett must think she was crazy. "I don't want to change."

When she looked up, her cheeks were damp and she was sure her makeup had smudged. Thankfully, she'd worn a waterproof mascara since crying after a family dinner wasn't exactly the most uncommon occurrence. She wasn't sad, more frustrated. Incensed, even.

Maybe it's because you think they're right, deep down? You are stupid. You can't pick the right men, you can't get your career off the ground. You're stuck and stagnant and you make bad decisions.

Beckett's expression was impossible to read, as usual. He closed his laptop and stashed it away, and then he turned to her with cool blue eyes focused intently on her face.

God, he must think that she was some hysterical crybaby.

McKenna went to leave but he leaned forward, his large, capable hands taking the bowl of ice cream from her and placing it on the coffee table next to his.

What she wouldn't give to have those hands on her—caressing her, learning her. Reassuring her.

"Some people aren't meant to fit into a box," he said.

The tears threatened again, but she fought them back. There was still time to get out of here with the last of her dignity intact. It might only be a shred, but it was hers and she needed it. She held his gaze for a moment before attempting to stand. But Beckett's hand reached for hers and she stilled. Frozen.

"If they can't see what a kind and creative person you are, then fuck 'em."

McKenna blinked. She hadn't ever heard Beckett swear before, and it took her by surprise. But now that she looked closer, his expression wasn't so hard to read after all. His eyes were like blue fire—shimmering and flickering with intensity. His mouth pressed into a hard line, his jaw ticking with effort. And his fingers wrapped around her wrist, burning through the thin fabric of her top.

He was angry. For her.

No one had ever been angry on her behalf before.

Her breath stuck in her throat. "Fuck 'em?"

"Fuck 'em."

He was closer now. When had that happened? While she was crying into her ice cream? The couch suddenly seemed small, like it was pushing them together.

"Maybe they're right," she said, a lump clogging her throat. "Maybe I am wasting my potential."

They hadn't said that exactly, but the message had been clear. Though whether it was because they thought her capable of more or because they simply couldn't conceive that someone who shared their DNA wasn't a genius, McKenna wasn't sure.

"What do you want to do?" he asked.

I want to kiss you.

No. Wrong answer.

But the thought hovered and tendrils of desire wound through her. Her breath hissed out between her lips like a silent *yes*. She wanted him. Badly.

"I…" She shook her head, trying to see through the fog. But it didn't work. "I…"

She shifted on the couch, digging her knees into the soft, comfortable cushions so that she was closer to him. Her head and heart couldn't align, the mixed signals clashing until it was all white noise.

"I don't know," she whispered, reaching her hand out to touch his face. His skin was soft, cleanly shaven. And damn he smelled incredible—like cologne and fresh cotton. "Or maybe I do."

"McKenna." His breath was warm against her palm, and she brushed her fingertip over the corner of his mouth.

He was still holding her other hand captive, like her touch had frozen him solid. But he wasn't retreating, wasn't backing away. Maybe he wanted it, too…?

The force with which his lips crashed down on hers took her by surprise, but she yielded. Quickly. Completely. He threaded one hand into the hair at the back of her head, cupping her skull. It was incredibly intimate. Possessive. He pushed his tongue between her lips and she almost groaned when it made contact with her own.

He was soft and hard. Demanding and coaxing. Perfect.

"God, Beckett." She leaned into him, struggling to balance as the couch shifted.

He pulled her into his lap, her knees digging into the cushions on either side of his couch. Something pressed against her hip—a cushion. He dug it out and tossed it onto the floor. There was nothing now but the two of them, lined up front to front. The contact sent her heartbeat skyrocketing and she flattened her palms on his chest, moving them up and down so she could feel every ridge of muscle. When she caught the hem of his jumper, sliding her palm over bare skin, he rocked against her.

Holy smokes the man could kiss. She'd expected it to be good—dreamed that it would be hot. But this was something else entirely. Something so right, a feeling of completeness wound through her. Settling her.

*Un*settling her.

Smooth skin rubbed against her neck as he nuzzled her. "You smell like cake."

His arm snaked around her waist, drawing her closer still, as she tipped her face to him. The coaxing of his lips had her humming with pleasure, but that soft sound turned to a gasp when he rolled his hips against that sweet spot between her legs. He was hard as a rock and the knowledge that she had him so turned on shot through her like a bullet.

Instinctively, she reached down and brushed her fingers along the length of him. The hard ridge of his cock strained against his jeans. Holy freaking crap. Mr. Whopper had *nothing* on Beckett Walsh.

Her fingertip toyed with the tab of his silver zipper, hovering as her head and heart duked it out. Well, her head and her lady-parts, more accurately. Turns out self-imposed celibacy was a lot harder than McKenna had anticipated. No pun intended.

The sound of "Sexy and I Know It" blasted into the air and McKenna jumped, startled. Only one person had that song assigned as their ringtone: Emery.

What the hell are you doing? Kissing a guy who's supposed to be engaged is not *part of the plan. Doesn't matter if he's the best kisser of all time who also happens to be hung like a freaking donkey…*

"Oh God," she muttered, shaking her head. "We should not be doing this."

She pushed back, scrambling to get off Beckett, who was looking just as shell-shocked as she felt. He didn't say a thing. That stoic, impersonal expression was back. His mask.

"I'm sorry, I…" She pushed up off the couch and bumped into the coffee table, wincing as the wood smacked her shin. "I should go."

For a moment it looked as though he might try to stop her. He rose from the couch, his sandy hair a mess from where her fingers had threaded and tugged and gripped it. But those blue eyes were no longer fire, they were hard and smooth and impenetrable as stone. His lips parted, but he snapped them shut, making a noise of acknowledgment instead. Great, so they were back to the grunting thing again.

What a bloody disaster. Unsure what to say, she turned on her heel and headed for the front door.

The only way you're going to get over this guy is to make sure his ex comes back. Starting tomorrow, Operation Self-Love is on hold. Operation Get Beckett Engaged Again is priority number one.

Chapter Eleven

Beckett rubbed his palms up and down his face, hoping that maybe if he did it enough times he might find the energy to tackle his problems. He wasn't the kind of guy to dwell on the negative—no matter what his sister claimed. He was a realist. A fact guy. A logical thinker with a problem-solving attitude.

But today he couldn't seem to get his head in the game. After staring blankly at the code he'd written first thing that morning and wondering why the hell his application had stalled, he finally saw the error. He'd forgotten to close a loop. Rookie mistake. It was coding 101, and something he would usually have caught with ease.

But not today. It felt as though his brain had taken a leave of absence.

At least he knew why…not that it made him feel any better. But the second McKenna had sent over an email with the subject line *Operation Get Beckett Engaged Again*, his brain had turned to mush.

He swiped his hand across his desk, disturbing a bunch of papers with his handwritten notes and sending a pen flying across the room. Bloody hell. Why was he feeling like he wanted to put a fist through a wall? That wasn't like him, at all.

"Kissing the girl next door isn't like you, either," he muttered.

But he had. He'd kissed McKenna like he'd been doing it his whole life, and been quite sure he'd died and gone to heaven. She'd tasted like vanilla and sugar, and smelled even sweeter. And her body…. Every curve and dip had been like silk under his palms.

Which was *not* how he was supposed to feel.

But that story about her family had gotten to him. He could practically feel their judgment, and seeing the tears shimmer in her eyes…fuck. Not cool. Something primal had roared up within him, a desire to protect. To defend. It was nothing like he'd ever experienced before.

But that wasn't supposed to happen. He wanted Sherri, not McKenna.

So why, then, did it feel like he'd been crushed by an avalanche when her email came through? There was no denying the bitter taste in the back of his throat. Nor the instinctive curl in his fists.

<From: Mac-K@youremail.com>
<To: B.Walsh@ M.K-Technologies.com>

Hi Beckett,

I was thinking about how to help you reconnect with your ex. I don't want to slack on my end of our bargain, so I've put together a four-point plan.

Make contact – This is a text or email to begin with, to test the waters. I can help you write this.

Face-to-face meeting – plan a meeting that shows

how well you know her (I'm thinking a restaurant that she loves or some other special spot.)

Give her a chance to have her say – it's natural to want to defend yourself, but this is her time to air her concerns.

Make a commitment – this needs to be concrete. Maybe it means ensuring you make time to have dinner with her on a certain night every week and you don't break that for anything. Give her the same thing you give your family.

Let's catch up and I can help you with step one.

McKenna.

A four-point plan on how to make contact like a normal human being? He wasn't sure whether to laugh or yell. Sure, he'd asked her for help. But telling him to email and give Sherri space to talk…did McKenna think he was a fucking Neanderthal?

Add that to the pile of bullshit he was already dealing with—complete radio silence from Sherri's father, the fact that Greg was back on the scene, and Kayla's tearful phone call earlier that morning, which proved he was right about her feeling unloved by her father—and he wanted nothing more than to bar his front door and commit to a life of solitude. The buzzing in his head was an incessant drone, preventing him from being able to think about anything for more than a minute before his brain bounced back to that kiss.

That all-consuming, so-bloody-wrong-it-was-right kiss.

Shaking his head to dislodge the vision of McKenna straddling him, her bright blue eyes sucking him in, he reached for his phone. The text area under Sherri's name was a single unanswered blue bubble from over a week ago.

Beckett: I know you're pissed, but we can work this out.

He needed to get his head back in the game. A detour with McKenna wasn't part of his plan and the kiss could be explained away. McKenna had been hurting and he'd wanted to comfort her. Sure, he should have stuck to ice cream and consoling words. It had gotten a bit out of control. But it didn't mean anything.

He wanted Sherri back in his life. He wanted everything to go back to how it had been a month ago. He vowed to himself that he would make it up to Sherri. McKenna was right, a dinner a week that he didn't break for anything was what he should have *already* been doing.

A jittering energy rippled through him and he pushed up so abruptly from his desk chair that he almost tipped it over. For so long, his life had been the stable, constant thing he needed—steady, interesting work, steady relationship, steady family. Now it was all going to hell and he wanted to scream until his lungs burned.

He glanced at clock above his desk. Five p.m. He hadn't eaten all day because he'd basically glued himself to his desk. Not that it made a lick of difference. The app had stalled… just like everything else.

To make matters worse, he'd been dodging calls from a prominent tech reporter who wanted to interview him about the new project. It was an opportunity he would have leaped on a few months ago, but now it felt like salt in the wound. If Beckett didn't fix things with Lionus, then he was doomed— by the time he found a new investor someone else might've beat him to the punch. In this industry, if you couldn't move quickly why even bother?

All his issues felt like they were layered on top of him, each negative thought increasing the pressure on his shoulders. The only joy he'd had since this whole thing blew up was when he was with McKenna.

"You should be with someone who excites you."

God, since when did he start taking relationship advice from his mother? After Beckett's father died, Minnie went on a rebound and never bounced back. She let a man walk in and out of her life, using her when he felt like it, and discarding her the rest of the time.

McKenna excites you.

It wasn't only her incredible curves and flirty smile that came to mind. It was her laugh, the crinkle that formed in her button nose whenever she was trying to figure him out. It was her uniqueness, her spark.

He swallowed. No, it was simple, red-blooded animal attraction and that was all. McKenna was beautiful, playful, sexy. Who *wouldn't* be attracted her? But physical chemistry wouldn't sustain a relationship. He needed stability. He needed someone who wanted the same things in life, someone with whom he shared more than a sizzling connection.

Sure, he was attracted to McKenna. But he wanted to be with Sherri. And that's what he had to focus on.

He glanced back at his computer, knowing that he should keep working. Keep pushing. But it was obvious he needed to clear the air with McKenna, otherwise he wasn't going to get anything done.

• • •

All day McKenna had oscillated between being angry at herself for kissing Beckett and wanting to storm down the hallway and pound on his door until she could see him again. Every word of the email she'd written to him had been like another needle in her skin. The four-point plan was pathetic, but she had to do *something.* Anything.

She wanted to push him away. Or rather, she wanted to protect herself. Because the more she got to know Beckett, the more she was convinced that his ex was an idiot to let him go. That beneath a stoic and sometimes gruff exterior was a kind, smart, passionate man. The kind of man she wanted… but who never seemed to want her.

"Hey." Isla reached out and touched her arm. "You're really out of it tonight."

Emery made a noise of agreement. "You're like the walking dead, right now."

McKenna sighed. "Tell me about it."

She looked down at the table where they'd spread out a bunch of makeup. Every six months the CAM-Ready Cosmetics staff got their "gratis," which was basically a ton of free makeup. But McKenna's drawers were overflowing and her freelance kit was full to the brim, so she let Emery and Isla come over and pick through her collection.

"Want to talk about it?" Isla cocked her head, her fair brows crinkled.

"I don't think it would help, to be honest." She sighed and reached for a lipstick in a funky silver tube, half-heartedly swiping it on the back of her hand. "I need to make peace with the fact that I'll never be able to make good decisions for myself."

Isla reached past her and grabbed a pale-pink blush in a heart-shaped container. "Career or love?"

"Career, love, family." She sighed. "All of the above. Not that you would understand, Little Miss Perfect."

McKenna had meant it as a joke, an attempt to lighten the mood, but her friend frowned. "You really think that?"

"Umm, who *doesn't* think that?" Emery scoffed.

"What did you call me, Em?" Isla tapped a fingertip to her chin. "A deranged Stepford wife in the making?"

"I kid because I love." Emery shrugged.

"Oh, and she's one hundred percent jealous," McKenna said, shooting her friend a knowing look as she pulled the top off another lipstick. "I am, too. You're getting married to a guy who adores you. Your job is awesome. And the worst thing is, we can't even hate you because you're just a kind, generous person. You make me sick."

"And what about me, huh?" Emery planted her hands on her hips. "Where's my string of compliments?"

"You're prickly as a cactus and twice as stubborn." She nudged Emery with her elbow, making sure she knew that—despite the truth—the ribbing was well-intentioned. But her friend's expression was a little misty. "But I love you anyway."

"Did I ever tell you I was engaged once before?" Isla asked.

McKenna blinked. "No. I had no idea."

"I left him at the altar." She toyed with the magnetic closure on an eyeshadow palette, her gaze fixed on nothing in particular. "I was all dressed up in this big, expensive gown. Vera Wang, of course, because that's what I thought I had to have. My hair and makeup were done. The bridesmaids had all gone to sort out an issue with the groomsmen. They left me alone for five minutes and I ran like a bat out of hell."

"Why?"

"Cold feet, I guess. It was like a total out of body experience." She laughed bitterly. "The truth is, I wasn't sure if he was the one. But he ticked all the boxes, and I didn't know why I had this gut feeling that something wasn't right… but I did."

"You made the right call." Emery nodded solemnly.

"What happened?" McKenna shook her head, shocked by Isla's very un-Isla-like revelation *and* the fact that Emery had never told her. "You just left the church?"

"Yup. I snuck out in my dress and made it all the way to the parking lot before Em spotted me." She pressed her fingertips to her temple, her enormous engagement ring flashing like a star. Emery, for once, was without a sarcastic response. Instead, she rubbed her sister's back in slow circles. "They tried to talk me into walking down the aisle but I couldn't do it. I've never felt like more of a failure in my whole life."

If Isla had made that kind of mistake, then what the hell kind of hope did anyone else have? This was the woman whose birth certificate likely read: Isla "I've got my shit together" Richardson.

"So now I've spilled my secret," Isla said. "How about you tell me what's going on with you?"

McKenna sighed. "I went off track with Operation Self-Love."

"How off track?" Emery pushed her glasses up over the bridge of her nose. "Are we talking a misdemeanor or a full-blown pre-meditated violation?"

"A misdemeanor. Let's call it reckless kissing."

"Under the influence?"

"No, I can't even blame it on being drunk. I'd come back from dinner with my parents and I was sober as a judge." She spun a lipstick around, watching the light catch on the grooves in the gold casing. "I'd had a really crappy day and Beckett was there, being all sweet and sexy. He even designed a new website for my business without me asking him to, and he told me he believes in me."

"He sounds really sweet." Isla frowned. "Is it so bad that you kissed him? I mean, in the grand scheme of things? I get why you want to do this whole 'self-love' thing, but it doesn't have to be a hard and fast rule."

"He's the guy I'm helping to get his ex back."

Isla pressed her lips together. "Oh."

"And I found out that one of the reasons he wants her back is because her father is funding his startup."

Emery raised a brow. "So he's into her because she's rich?"

She drummed her fingers against her knee. "You know, every time I think that…it just…doesn't feel right. It doesn't feel like him."

"What do you mean?"

"He seems like a genuinely good person. He cares about his family, he's passionate about his work." She huffed. "He's not a loser deadbeat in the making like some of the guys I've dated—but he's not a pretentious dickhead, either."

"So you kissed him. What changes?"

"That's the thing, I don't know. I hightailed it out his apartment after it happened. Real mature." She rolled her eyes. "And then this morning I sent him a four-point plan on how he can get his ex back."

Isla cringed. "Did he respond?"

"I haven't heard a peep from him all day."

"What do you *want* to happen?" Emery asked with a pointed look, as though she already knew the answer.

McKenna had learned a long time ago that wanting was a dangerous thing, because it set you up for failure. The second you admitted you wanted something, not getting that thing made you feel like a piece of crap. But in her quest to do her own thing—and to avoid feeling disappointed in herself, since she got enough of that shit from her family—she'd apparently set the bar so low she tripped over it on the way to her front door each morning.

She'd been stuck in her retail job for several years, only now taking a leap to build her freelance business when she should have been doing it from the start. But fear of failure had kept her stagnant.

Maybe that was why she always chose the wrong men. Either picking ones who weren't her type so she wouldn't feel bad when they broke up, or aiming for someone too perfect so she wouldn't give herself the chance to get attached. But Beckett didn't fall into either of those categories. He wasn't perfect, far from it. But he had all the things that attracted her: ambition, intelligence, and personal quirks that made him interesting. Not to mention that the packaging was spot on.

"It wasn't a trick question," Emery said, nudging McKenna with her elbow.

"I want him," she whispered, hating herself for not being able to deny it.

Dammit. This wasn't supposed to happen. She was supposed to be worrying about herself, focusing on her work and taking a break from the cycle of relationship failure.

Who says it has to fail?

The whisper may as well have been the roar of a typhoon. Because now she'd admitted it aloud, there was no taking it back.

"I know I shouldn't. He's supposed to be engaged to someone else…"

"But he's not," Emery pointed out. "She called things off, correct? They are officially broken up."

"Right."

"And he hasn't seen her in that time?"

"No." She shook her head. "Not to my knowledge."

"Then you haven't done anything wrong and neither has he." Isla placed a reassuring hand on her shoulder. "Don't beat yourself up for this."

"But I feel so guilty." McKenna dropped her head into her hands. "God, why am I so stupid?"

"You're not stupid. There's obviously chemistry between you two, or you wouldn't be feeling like this," Isla said.

"And so what?" Emery threw her hands up in the air. "Sorry to be the blunt one, as usual, but she dumped him. It's *finito*. Over. Donesky."

Isla rolled her eyes. "Yeah, we get it, Em."

"Ergo he's single," Emery said. "So what the hell is the problem?"

The memory of her body sparking under his touch shot through her, burning her up. "He still wants to be with her, not me."

"Do you think he goes around building websites for everyone?" Emery asked. "From what you've said, the guy barely speaks two words unless he's forced to, but suddenly you're going to his place for ice cream."

"Talk to him," Isla said. "If he kissed you, then he must feel something. But if he's still hung up on the ex then walk away."

The thought of cutting ties with Beckett made her stomach flip, and not in the good way. Lately, seeing him had been the highlight of her day. Watching his serious expression morph into a crooked grin when she said something funny, seeing the anger in his eyes on her behalf…it made her feel desired. Cared for.

Which was more than she could say for any of her exes.

"You're right." She bobbed her head. "I'll talk to him and clear the air. I don't want to go on not knowing if these feelings are mutual. It's sad, but…with most other guys I could take them or leave them. But I really like him."

That was the difference. Breaking up with Gage had dented her ego. But losing Beckett would dent something far more important—her heart.

"Then it's worth exploring. But don't let him think he can have his cake and eat it, too." Isla slung an arm around her shoulders. "You deserve better than that."

McKenna swallowed, a fluttering sensation like the beating of butterfly wings filling her with nervous energy. "Yeah, I do."

The women pushed up from their chairs and grabbed

their bags. "We should get going," Isla said. "I promised Mum I'd go with her to look at some outfit options for the rehearsal dinner and I'm dragging this one along with me."

"Ugh." Emery rolled her eyes and broke into a laugh when her sister pretended to strangle her.

"Have fun." McKenna leaned over the table to tidy the makeup, slotting each item back into their respective packages.

"We will." Isla laid a hand gently on McKenna's shoulder. "And if you need to chat or vent about the guy thing, you know I'm here for you."

"Same here." Emery leaned in and gave her a quick hug.

"Thanks, ladies. I appreciate it."

She walked the two women to the front door and waited while they grabbed their coats and scarves, bundling themselves up to face the cold.

"Let me know how it goes," Isla said. "I'm going to be an old married woman soon, so I need to live vicariously."

"Ha. Consider yourself lucky that you don't have to go through this anymore." McKenna pulled the door open. "It's not easy."

"What's not easy?" The male voice made McKenna jump and she found herself pinned by Beckett's laser-like blue gaze.

"Uhh…" McKenna's brain sputtered.

"Looks like that's our cue to leave," Emery said, mouthing "call me" once she was out of Beckett's field of vision.

He stood in her doorway, dressed in jeans and a T-shirt, which had "if at first you don't succeed, call it beta version 1.0" printed in white letters. Is that what this was? A test?

He planted his palm against the wooden frame of her door. "We need to talk."

Chapter Twelve

This was a first for Beckett. The words "we need to talk" had never before left his lips. He'd discovered early on that those four little words were woman-code for trouble. No matter who said them—his mother, his sister, or Sherri—it never ended well.

But if he didn't clear his head of all things McKenna, there was no way he'd be able to get back into his work. And if he couldn't work…then what the hell was the point of any of this?

"Never thought I'd hear *you* say that," she said. She hadn't invited him in yet, nor had she shrunk back from the way he leaned toward her. "Now, if you said we need to grunt about it on the other hand…"

"You know me so well," he drawled.

"I do, don't I?" This time there wasn't any sarcasm in her voice—no teasing, no deflection. Just raw vulnerability.

That, combined with her bare face—which he didn't think he'd ever seen—and her dressed-down outfit of an oversized blue *My Little Pony* hoodie and leggings, made her look stripped. Exposed.

"You have freckles," he said, his eyes narrowing. "I've never seen them before."

As much as he thought McKenna looked beautiful with her sparkly eyelids and fringy lashes, he liked her this way, too. Maybe because it made him think of how she might look in the morning—fresh faced and disheveled.

Stop that right now.

"I get them on my shoulders and my arms, too, come summer time." Her lips quirked. "Come on, get out of the hallway before people start gossiping."

He walked into her apartment and she shut the door behind him, flicking the lock. The loud *click* echoed in her quiet apartment. This was the first time he'd been inside… and it was so perfectly her. A little messy, bright and welcoming. Makeup was strewn all over a small white dining table. A pink couch faced a small TV and was littered with mismatched cushions in shades of purple and blue. Some had sequins on them, others were made of velvet or silk. And the place smelled like vanilla cupcakes.

The pulse of desire that shot through his body, causing a tightness in his muscles—and behind the fly of his jeans— shook him. "I want to talk about your email," he blurted out a little harsher than anticipated.

Smooth moves, Walsh. Why don't you bark at her next time?

"What did you think of the plan?" she asked. Her fingers tugged at the hem of her hoodie, picking at a loose thread.

"I wasn't sure if it was a serious suggestion or not."

She fidgeted as he studied her, silent. For once, her mouth wasn't running a mile a minute and he desperately wanted to know her game plan. It felt like they were two dogs circling one another, neither one ready to make the first move.

"What do you want me to say?" she asked, shaking her

head. "I'm trying to do the right thing."

The right thing was drawing a line in the sand. Pushing him away. He swallowed. Logically, she was right. Logically, he agreed with her. But, for once, he wanted to tell logic to go and fuck itself. He wanted McKenna. Wanted to throw all his rules and overthinking and rigidity out the window and just live.

You should be with someone who excites you.

Those words were stuck on repeat. It was like a glass shattering into a million pieces. It couldn't be reversed. He couldn't un-think that thought.

No, that's not *what you want. You have control here.*

Maybe he'd been stifling his life this whole time, by being too worried about financial security. By being too worried about making sure his mother had everything she needed because he thought it was his responsibility to take care of her. By thinking that work was the only thing he was good at.

But since he and McKenna had made their pact, he hadn't thought so little about his work in his whole life. She distracted him. Made him question the things he thought he wanted.

That's not a good thing. You need to be focused. Stay on track!

But his control was evaporating, drifting like smoke through his fingers so that no matter how hard he tried to grasp it, he couldn't. *That's* what she did to him. McKenna made normal things feel different. She'd turned everything on its head.

She made him ask questions he wasn't sure he wanted to know the answer to.

"What's the right thing?" he asked, taking a step forward.

Her eyes widened, and her shoulders rose as she sucked in a breath. "Sticking to the plan."

"The four-point plan?"

"Yeah." She nodded. "You want Sherri back and I agreed to help you."

Did he want Sherri back? He swallowed. His head said yes. The whole thing had started with McKenna because he'd wanted to get back to how things were before—stable. Secure.

But if he was being honest with himself—with her—his heart said no.

Guilt rocketed through him. In his quest to chase the things that had been so lacking in his childhood, he'd been chasing the wrong woman for all the wrong reasons. And not only did he deserve better than that…she did, too.

"What if I decided I don't want your help anymore?" he asked.

"Look, I know the plan might not have seemed that good. But—"

"Screw the plan, McKenna."

He was sick of it—sick of acting like he wasn't attracted to her. Sick of pretending that everything could go back to normal. Normal was gone and he felt…free.

• • •

"Don't." The words stuck in her throat.

God, why was this man so hard to resist? If his ex couldn't see what a great guy he was, then she was blind and she didn't deserve him.

"Don't what?" Concern laced his tone. She swallowed and stayed stock-still.

"You don't have to keep pretending like you're attracted…"

She couldn't force herself to finish the sentence. Because he'd shown again and again that he *was* attracted to her. From that time in the elevator, to their bungled test date, to their white-hot kiss last night. But that wasn't enough to make things work between them. He wanted another woman.

No matter how much she wanted him, she'd never *ever* use her family's money to lure a guy in. That's why she wasn't supposed to fall for him, because then she wouldn't have to face his shattering rejection. She could simply skip off into the sunset by herself—dignity intact. Go back to her original plans for Operation Self-Love. Back to creating her own happiness.

But even with Kayla's wedding looming—the one thing she needed to get her business off the ground and take steps to have the success she craved—she felt empty at the thought of losing him.

You never had him to begin with.

"Keep pretending that I'm attracted to *you*?" He couldn't mask the hurt in his voice. "Keep pretending like I enjoy spending time with you? Do you really think this is all an act?"

"No." Her voice was small.

How was she supposed to tell him that she'd crossed the line? Well, mentally anyway. He thought they were friends and she wanted…more.

If he only wants to be friends, then why is he here?

"I know it's not an act." She walked over to the couch and dropped down, hugging a throw pillow to her chest. "But I know we're not… God. I don't know what I'm doing."

"We're talking." His Adam's apple bobbed, and his expression belied the cool, calm, and collected tone of his voice.

He feels it, too.

The couch shifted as he sat next to her. This time, neither of them left a gap in the middle. He was right there, his thigh touching hers. Impossibly close. Her breath hitched. The feeling of wanting had started small—like a bare spark—until it swept through her, a blazing inferno of anticipation.

"Is that all? And don't hide behind all that literal stuff. I know that's a front."

He *was* a literal guy. But she knew now his silence and matter-of-fact way hid a passion so bright and so hot that it made every other man she'd been with pale in comparison.

"What do you want me to say?" He raked a hand through his hair. "This is unchartered territory."

She didn't want to hope that he might see something more in her than all the other guys she'd dated. Guys like Gage, who thought she was fun but lacking in substance. Hoping was dangerous and she'd been let down too many times before. By her exes, who thought she had nothing more to offer than flirting and flings. By her parents, who wanted to change her.

By herself, for quietly listening to all the insults and swallowing them like bitter little pills and allowing herself to be frightened of failure.

"Tell me I'm not the only one feeling something here." Her breath stuttered in and out. "Take the pressure off, Beckett. Tell me the truth."

A noise vibrated in the back of his throat—dark and animalistic.

"Please." Her heart galloped. "I need to know this isn't you scratching an itch because you're lonely and nursing a bruised ego."

For once, Beckett wasn't able to hide behind his mask of impassivity. He wasn't the logical, literal guy who made decisions based on calculations. A kaleidoscope of emotion shifted on his face—the war going on inside telling her that she *wasn't* the only one feeling confused right now.

"Tell me." She reached up and touched his cheek, her fingertips catching on the golden stubble that'd broken through his skin. "I don't want to be your rebound girl."

Beckett crashed his mouth down on hers, knocking the

air from her lungs with one desperate, no-holds-barred kiss. McKenna's hands curled into his T-shirt, holding him close as he pressed down against the couch. It was so wrong—he was supposed to want someone else, but satisfaction barreled through her as he groaned into her mouth.

No amount of reasoning could hold her back now. Not when his hands were tangled in her hair, his lips open and hard against hers. His large frame felt even bigger as he covered her, his leg wedged between hers.

"McKenna." His teeth tugged at her earlobe, his stubble rasping against the sensitive skin on her neck. "What you do to me…"

"Yes." The word hissed out between her teeth, her chest rising and falling with anticipation. "Tell me."

"Words are inadequate to describe you."

She melted into him. Never before had a man said so little and affected her so much. But that was Beckett in a nutshell. Unconventional. Quiet. Perfect.

"Bedroom," she growled. "Now."

They stumbled off the couch and she dragged him to her room, her fingers interlaced with his. Her room was what she liked to call structured chaos, which meant that even though it looked a little crazy, she knew where everything was. On another day, she might hastily try to create some order knowing that he was her opposite—clean, minimal, orderly— but right then she didn't care.

She only cared about having him. Now.

"Undress for me," he said, his voice strained.

She stripped her Rainbow Dash hoodie over her head. The leggings came next, landing in a soft *whomp* on the carpeted floor.

"Bloody hell." The awe in Beckett's voice sent goose bumps rippling across her skin. "You're magnificent."

McKenna felt as though her knees had suddenly turned

to jelly. How did he manage to do that to her? He could strip her back to her most basic desires with only a few words, like he'd somehow tapped into the very core of her. Like he knew *exactly* what she needed.

"Leave the rest." His eyes swept over her, taking in the neon-pink lace of her bra and underwear. A set that made her feel good and was never supposed to be seen by him.

Yeah right. Like you didn't wish for this very moment...

Oh, she'd wished, all right. But there'd never been any planning where Beckett was concerned. This was entirely *off* plan.

She climbed onto the bed and let her head sink back against her pillow. Her fingertips caught on the embroidery of her bedspread, trying to keep her calm for what was about to come next. Her hand extended out toward him.

"Aren't you going to undress?" she asked, excitement and anxiety warring inside her.

"Soon." The bed shifted as Beckett hovered over her.

His eyes were consumed by the black of his pupils, his brows knitted and his nostrils flaring. The intensity in his expression made her breath come faster as he studied her. Watched her. Scrutiny was something she avoided, but he'd pinned her with only his gaze.

"I want to see you," she said. When he was quiet like this, she felt her own words bubbling up to the surface. The noise was her protection from the criticism in her head. From the worry that maybe he didn't like what he was seeing, that maybe she should have done something better with her hair. Maybe she should have asked for a moment to freshen up...

"Soon," he repeated.

She swallowed. "Please. I want to see what's underneath."

"You have," he said. He pressed his lips over hers, the kiss far too chaste for what she'd imagined. For what she wanted to do, now.

"What are—"

"Shhh." A crooked, charming grin tugged at his lips. "Always talking."

"One of us has to." She bit down on her lip.

"Why?" His hand had come to her breast, his fingers tracing the scalloped edging of her bra as if committing the shape to memory.

"How else are we supposed to know what one another is thinking if we're not talking?" She hummed in pleasure as he plucked her nipple straight through her bra. "You know, there's a biological reason why we speak. It's very important, and sometimes I worry when you don't say anything—"

"McKenna." Her name was soft and silky, like melted butter on his tongue. "Humans actually communicate most information nonverbally."

But that left things open to interpretation, and history had told her she wasn't too good at getting it right. She thought things were going well, and then they weren't. She thought someone liked her, but they didn't...or not in the same way that she liked them. Nonverbal communication was ambiguous, difficult. Dangerous.

"Are you going to tell me to shut up, then?" She felt vulnerable now. Raw and open and terrified that he could see how much she wanted this to be real because it was probably splashed all over her face. Maybe she *should* shut up. Because the more she spoke, the more she let him in.

"No." He shook his head. "You wouldn't be you without the chatter."

"Chatter?" It didn't sound like an insult when he said it.

"But I work better with actions than words," he said. His lips probed hers, dissolving her concerns. "Close your eyes."

She nodded, complying. Without her sight, everything else was amplified. Every other sense dialed up in intensity to compensate for the black behind her eyelids. She could hear things that maybe before would have gone unnoticed—the slight scratch of Beckett's jeans against the silky bedspread as he moved. Then his absence.

"Don't move." He sounded farther away.

Then there was footsteps and McKenna's heart hammered against her ribs. What if this was some cruel joke? What if he'd decided he didn't want her and now he was making a stealth exit while she lay there, waiting?

She was slowly freaking out over his rejection—anticipating it—but the press of something at her ear jolted her. She felt the familiar snug fit of her earbud headphones in one ear and the brush of his lips at her other.

"Just to prove that words aren't everything." His voice was raspy, ragged. "You can open your eyes now."

Without waiting for her response, he slipped the other bud into her ear. The drone of white noise filled her head with nothingness. For a moment, the lack of context made her anxious, but when cool air blew across her stomach she almost launched off the bed. Her eyes sprung open and the sight of his wide, wolfish smile was everything.

"This is…" She had no idea if he could hear her or not. "I want you, Beckett."

For some reason, not being able to hear her own voice above the sounds—and not waiting for a response from him—made her feel free. Uninhibited.

Then the rough edge of his jaw brushed against her skin. She let her eyes close again as she lay there, feeling him. Focusing on the intense pleasure of his touch. Teeth. Lips. Fingers. Silk. Her skin prickled with awareness, her nerves firing on all cylinders and making blood fizz in her veins. If he wasn't careful, he'd short circuit her brain before they got to the good stuff.

But that was exactly it. With Beckett, *everything* was the good stuff—it wasn't about ticking boxes and saying the right thing. Or going to the right places. Or wearing the right outfit.

She could simply be herself around him.

The slow-burn build-up, the teasing, the games were everything she never knew she wanted. She opened her mouth to say something, but decided against it, and she had no idea if he'd caught her almost-slip or not. He moved farther down her body, his tongue swiping across the skin lower on her belly, almost at the waistband of her underwear.

Yes. Lower. Please.

Chapter Thirteen

McKenna was a vision. Correction, she was *always* a vision. But today she was a vision from the depths of his desires, from the part he'd locked away the moment he'd met her in the hopes his needs might slink off into the night.

Her vibrant purple hair was splayed across the shiny satin pillow. Breath stuttered in and out of her open mouth. She'd closed her eyes, letting her dark lashes rest. But it was the winding trail of her white headphones down from her ears connected to his phone on the bedside table that was doing unspeakable things to him.

He used the app with the white noise to help him sleep on nights when every mistake he'd ever made swirled around in his head. Never once had he thought it would serve a purpose other than sleep. But he needed to show her how he felt, rather than say it.

Because words were not his strong point. Never had been. He was a man of action, of decision. And sitting on her couch tonight, feeling happier than he ever had, told him something. Maybe his mother was right. There *was* more to life than chasing success. He craved the security that money afforded him because he'd never been able to get it anywhere else.

But he had enough in the bank to get by. He could delay his project and do it on *his* terms—slower, smaller. Independently.

And that meant he could be here, now. Instead of chasing the thing he *thought* he should have. The thing that had never quite felt right, no matter how much he'd tried to make it so. He could have McKenna. Now. Tomorrow. Next week.

Until when…?

Why was his mind already jumping to the future instead of simply reveling in her mostly-naked body? He shook the thoughts out of his head. It was the thrill of being able to cut the strings from his wrists that had his head swirling with possibilities. A weight had been lifted from his shoulders.

He leaned back and allowed himself to watch her for a moment. The way she pressed her lips together and writhed, as though her body was so alive with anticipation that she couldn't stay still, made him grow impossibly hard. He rubbed a palm down the front of his jeans, trying to dispel some of the tension there, but nothing short of being inside her would relieve that need. Her eyes snapped open, as if she were trying to figure out where he'd gone.

"I'm not leaving you." He brushed his thumb over her lips and she smiled, the serene expression socking him straight in the chest. It was as if she understood him even though she couldn't hear his words.

As Beckett dragged the backs of his knuckles down over the patch of satin covering her sex, McKenna bucked. She was so beautifully responsive. So pliant.

"Don't worry," he said. "I'll take care of you."

He dragged the underwear down over her hips and she shifted, lifting herself so that he could undress her. Her knees immediately fell open in invitation. God, what had he done to deserve this? She was even more perfect for him than he'd ever let himself imagine.

Running his hands up the insides of her thighs, he leaned forward. At the first brush of his lips against her sex, she gasped.

"So sensitive." He blew cool air across her flushed skin and a tremor ran through her.

Her sex was slick, her breathing shallow, and every time he touched her she almost launched off the bed. Nuzzling the inside of her thigh, he breathed in the scent of her excitement. "We're not going to rush this."

He wanted to learn every inch of her body. From the delicate bones at the base of her neck, to the tiny little mole hidden in the crook of her elbow. He traced the dip at her waist with his fingertips, loving how her body flared back out again over her hips and thighs.

All the while, her eyes followed him. Her shiny, pink lips parted with each gasp, with each kiss he planted on her body. For once no words came out—but that didn't mean she was quiet. And thank God. Every gasp and mewl shot fire through his veins, stoking the burning desire that he'd been trying so hard to douse with logic and reasoning.

But there was nothing reasonable about being with McKenna.

He crawled up her body and drew one perfect, pink nipple into his mouth. Gently at first, and then harder, he sucked and rolled the sensitive tip between his teeth. Her hands flew to his head, her nails dragging against his scalp.

"Yes," she moaned, her eyes screwed shut.

Was this what it was like with her? Every sensation was dialed up to ten. Her skin was silk under his palms, her lips soft and warm when he hovered over her for a delving kiss, groaning when her hips rolled up to brush against where his cock strained against the fly of his jeans.

Her blue eyes sparkled as she hooked her fingers into the waistband of his jeans, showing him what she wanted rather than telling.

"Not yet."

He had to taste her first. *All* of her.

His hands pushed her thighs even farther apart, pinning her legs to the bed. There was no hesitation when he brought his lips to her, no tentative exploration or gentle loving. He was direct and focused his attention right on that sensitive bundle of nerves at her clit. McKenna wasn't able to remain quiet then; her cries filled his head as she came hard and fast against his mouth, her hips rolling and thrusting up until she'd wrung ever drop of pleasure from her orgasm.

Yes.

The word hissed in his brain, like steam escaping a pot of boiling water. Being with her felt so right. So perfectly right.

He traced circles on the inside of her thigh as she came down from the edge of bliss, joining the dots of the freckles and moles that were scattered like cinnamon across her fair skin.

"You undo me," he said.

He found himself moving back up to her sex, desperate to taste her again. She writhed beneath him, still sensitive, but the squeak in her throat turned gravelly and breathy. Thighs trembling, she sank her teeth into her lower lip and Beckett had to force himself to concentrate on her lest he finish himself before he'd even got started. He dragged another orgasm from her and this time it was slow and sensual, the tremors lasting longer, her thighs quaking as they clamped against his head.

He eased her legs down and pushed up on his palms. The way she looked at him—eyes heavy lidded with arousal, lips open as she panted—was everything. Leaning forward, he gently tugged the earbuds from her ears.

"I want you to hear this, McKenna," he said, whispering the words close to her ear. "You've got me so fucking wound up seeing you all laid out like that. I want to be inside you."

Her lip trembled. "I want that, too."

Standing, he tore his T-shirt over his head. The delicate muscles in her neck moved as she swallowed, and McKenna propped herself up to watch. He tugged on the belt at his waist, freeing it from the clasp and then he slowly drew his fly down. Her eyes tracked every movement.

"More," she said.

He stuck his thumbs into the waistband of his jeans and pulled them down. Then he stripped off his socks and left them with the growing heap of clothing on her floor.

She sucked on the inside of her cheek. "Can I do the last bit?"

When he nodded, she crawled over the bed on all fours and knelt in front of him, looking up. The sharp angle made her blue eyes seem even wider and deeper. He could drown here, standing on the ground without a drop of water in sight. Her fingers brushed over his erection, tracing him through the fabric of his boxer briefs from root to tip. He stifled a moan in the back of his throat as pure, undulated pleasure filtered through him like a drug.

McKenna peeled his waistband down and his cock bobbed up against his stomach. Underwear forgotten, her hands came to him. Stroking, teasing, cupping.

"God, McKenna," he ground the words out.

She left him momentarily to reach into the drawer beside her bed, and he pulled his boxer briefs completely off. When she produced a foil packet, he held out his hand but McKenna shook her head.

"I want to do it." She tore the packet open and pulled out the condom, reaching for him with her free hand.

He'd never thought contraception to be something sexy, but the way McKenna rolled the rubber down his length, her fingers forming a tight ring around his cock, Beckett revised his position.

"You make everything feel good," he whispered.

Reaching for his hand, she leaned back against the bed and pulled him on top of her. "So do you."

He knelt between her legs and stroked her with his fingers, pumping one and then two inside her. Her back arched and her head lolled against her pillow, her features contorted with pleasure. No matter how much he wanted to string this out—to savor every damn second so that he could hold the memory bright and vivid in his mind—he was already at the edge. When his cock pushed into her, a feeling of completeness rocketed through him. It wasn't supposed to be right...but it was. He thrust slowly, giving her time to accommodate him, but the second she hummed in pleasure and her fingers curled around his biceps, he knew they would need to go for round two tonight.

There would be time for a long, slow, sensual fucking later. Right now, he needed to push them both over. Together.

"Don't hold back, okay?" Her lips brushed his ear. "I want it all."

All? What else was there but this?

Her hips swirled beneath his; she was talking with her body. Showing him what she wanted.

"I won't hold back," he gritted the words out as he thrust into her. His muscles tensed as she cried out his name. It was so much better than anything else she could have said, so much more powerful than any long-winded declaration. Any dirty talk. Any whispered demands.

Just his name, the edges cut with desire.

"Beckett," she groaned again and that final sound pushed him over the edge.

• • •

They'd lain, tangled in one another, until a sound broke the quiet of their even breathing. A rumble from McKenna's stomach.

"Hungry?" He propped himself up on one arm and brushed an errant strand of hair from her face.

The gesture was so intimate that McKenna blushed. Which seemed a little silly given what they'd done, but she wasn't used to hearts and romance around sex. Her ex had always immediately gone to shower afterward. Alone.

"Yeah. *Someone* distracted me." She couldn't help a blissful grin flaring across her lips. "It's okay. I'll consider this fasted cardio."

Beckett leaned forward and brushed a kiss over her cheek. "What do you want to eat?"

"Is it terrible if I say I want awful, so-bad-it's-good junk food?"

"Okay." He nodded and pushed up from the bed.

Naked, Beckett was even more glorious than she'd imagined. He was lean, athletic. Not chunky and built like a gym bro, but sleeker. Honed. An efficient machine. Pale golden hair dusted his legs, and made a trail from his belly button stretching down. He had a light smattering on his chest, too.

"You're staring," he said, cocking his head.

"Sure am." She grinned and made a move to get out of bed. But he stopped her, pushing her back down with a firm hand and a firmer kiss.

"I'll get it." He jerked his head toward the window. "It's raining."

Damn if her heart didn't melt into a puddle. A man who was incredibly unique and thoughtful in bed, and who was willing to brave crappy weather alone to get snacks…she'd stumbled across Mr. Perfect.

Instead of reveling in bliss, an uneasiness settled over her. She *never* found Mr. Perfect, let alone managed to convince him that she was *Miss* Perfect. Why would Beckett be any different?

He stepped into his jeans and pulled them up, tugging his belt tight at his waist. When he was fully dressed, he planted a kiss on her head and left without a word. Quiet, as ever. McKenna sighed and ran her hands over the embroidery on her bedspread, trying to ease the churning in her gut.

This was exactly what she wanted—a guy who was kind, sexy, intelligent. It seemed too good to be true. And he hadn't explicitly said that he was over his ex, had he? She bit down on her lip, trying to think back. He'd told her to "screw the plan" but that was it. Well, other than saying words were inadequate to describe her.

"Ugh." She thumped a fist down onto the bed. Why did this all have to be so complicated?

Her phone buzzed next to her bed, a message flashing up on the screen. It was darker now, silent except for the pitter-patter of rain, and the screen illuminated her bedside table.

Kayla: Hi McKenna! I would love to book you for my wedding makeup and for our rehearsal dinner, too. I'd love to treat my mother as well. Let me know if you're open to that and I'll send the details through.

Her heart leaped into her throat. Two jobs! This was even better than she could have hoped for. The money would be great, but more importantly, the potential exposure would be huge. She squealed and hugged her phone to her chest. This was it. Her big break.

By the time Beckett returned with their food—an assortment of calorie-laden goodies from a local burger joint—she was filled to bursting with excitement.

"Kayla wants me to do her makeup," she said, bouncing up and down on the couch as she not-so-patiently waited for him to extract all the food from the plastic bags, which were spotted with water. Much like Beckett himself. "I can't believe it. I mean, I *can*. But it's so exciting. Now I can put something on my website for…for, whatever those things are. Recommendations? Or are they accolades? Like those quote things, you know? Anyhow, do you think she'd want to give me one of those? I hope does. Oh, I'm so excited."

Beckett smiled and dumped a small paper bag of fries onto a plate that he'd collected from her kitchen. "Congratulations."

"Thanks." She reached for a fry. "I have been holding back on this for way too long. But no more! I'm going to make this business work and then I can finally quit working at CAM-Ready and work for myself. Just like you do." She looked over the food options and selected chicken nuggets and a cheeseburger. "What exactly do you do, anyway? I know it's computer programming and business stuff. But what are you working on now?"

He looked up at her, a brow raised. "You want to hear about my app?"

"Sure." She munched on a nugget. "I'm interested."

"Oh." He looked almost…confused. "Well, it's a wealth management app."

"What's it called?"

"WealthHack." He settled on the couch next to her and grabbed a burger for himself. "You sync the app to your online banking and investment accounts and it gives you reports on spending habits. You can set up alerts to help with budgeting and it provides daily reminders of your financial goals."

"WealthHack." She bobbed her head. "I like it. So it's basically a robot financial adviser?"

He chuckled. "Basically. The aim is for it to become something that financial institutions recommend to people for building better investing habits. But it can also be useful for people who are trying to work their way out of credit card and other types of bad debt, because the app is built to focus on habits. It learns how you spend to provide customized advice on where you can save money to then invest in something that will help you grow your wealth long term."

"I think that's the most I've heard you talk about anything," she teased.

He rolled his eyes, but didn't look upset.

"Seriously though, it's incredible." She placed a hand on his knee. "You're going to make millions. I can see so many people wanting an app like that."

He chewed, the excitement evaporating from his expression. "That's if we even see it to fruition."

McKenna concentrated on her meal, unsure whether to let on that she knew Sherri's father was supposed to be financially backing the project. But she didn't want to get Kayla in trouble for spilling the beans. "What do you mean?"

Moment of truth. Would he lie to her?

"Lionus Aldridge, Sherri's father, was planning to invest in WealthHack." He cleared his throat. "But he pulled out when Sherri and I broke up."

"Right."

It was so hard to tell what Beckett was thinking. He managed to hide his emotions away behind his clear, blue eyes and perfect mouth. There wasn't a telltale crease between his brows or a downturn of his mouth. Just a mask of neutrality.

"What happens now?" she asked.

He shook his head. "I don't know. Without that money, there's no way I'll get it to market by the date I'd set. I won't be able to pay the app developers or do any marketing activities. I've already lost the office space, because I wouldn't sign the lease without knowing if I had the funds to pay for it."

"Can't you find someone else to invest in it?"

"By then it could be too late, someone might beat me to the finish line." He sighed. "This business is so competitive and time sensitive. Losing funding at this stage is basically a death sentence."

It looked as though he was about to add something else, but instead he bit down on his burger. Her heart contracted for him. She couldn't even imagine how tough it must be to potentially wash so much work—and a fabulous idea—down the drain.

"Is that why you wanted to get back with Sherri?" The question popped out before she could stop it.

She expected him to bite back, to look hurt or upset. Or even to give her nothing. But he surprised her with a guilty twist of his mouth. "It certainly wasn't the whole reason. I *did* care about her and I wanted to marry her. At least, I thought I did. But I'd be lying if I didn't say that I needed her father's money."

"That's not a reason to be with someone." She put her food down, her appetite suddenly waning. "I don't know where this is going, but I can't promise—"

"Stop." He set his plate down and turned to her. "I'm not asking you for that."

She wanted to feel relieved. But uncertainty hung like a cloud overhead. This situation was messy. And emotional mess was not her forte, judging by how she handled her parents and their attitudes toward her. Her stomach twisted and turned.

But she'd asked a lot of Beckett already. And he hadn't held anything back. Maybe she should enjoy his company and take it slow with the personal stuff. Figure out what her next steps were before potentially jumping in with a "what do we call this?" conversation.

The silence strangled her. Beckett seemed to have retreated into his own head, and had abandoned his food also. Dammit. Why did she have to go and ruin a perfectly good evening with her questions? Maybe she *did* talk too much.

"Why don't we watch a movie?" she suggested, flashing him a bright smile. "I'm in the mood for something funny."

"Sure." He slid an arm along the back of the couch in invitation and she snuggled into his side, leaning her head against his chest.

She had no idea where they were headed, but something told her to take it slow. To watch her step. Since Operation Self-Love had been officially shelved, she needed a new mission. Operation Figure Out Beckett Walsh was now in effect.

Chapter Fourteen

The movie finished around midnight. McKenna had fallen asleep on him, her head nestled against his neck, the gentle in and out of her breath warming his skin. He'd picked her up, carried her to her bedroom, and gently placed her in bed. She mumbled something in a groggy voice, her arms clinging to his neck for a moment before he disentangled himself from her vice-like grip.

Despite all the worry and confusion battling in his head, this small gesture made him smile in the darkness. The girl wore her heart on her sleeve, that was for damned sure. And he liked it.

No head games. No playing hard to get.

He brushed the hair from her forehead and tugged the covers up over her. Light filtered in between the slats of her blinds, illuminating the shape of her in the bed. As tempting as it was to stay and spend the night wrapped up in her, he needed to get home and clear his head. The revelation about Sherri was playing on his mind. Not to mention that if he was accepting that Lionus's money wasn't going to come in, then he needed to start working on a Plan B.

With a light step, so as not to wake her, he left her room and closed the door with a soft snick. Then he grabbed the empty containers from their meal and stuffed them into one of the takeaway bags so he could drop them in the chute on the way back to his place. But the second he stepped outside her apartment, his eyes locked onto something unusual and everything else was forgotten.

"Mum?" He stalked toward the crumpled figure at the end of the hall.

His mother looked up, her eyes hooded and sleepy. Her skin blotchy. Tear-stained. "Beck?"

"What on earth are you doing here?" His gaze whipped around. She had a coat but nothing else.

"I tried to call you," she said.

Shit. He hadn't taken his phone to McKenna's, not expecting that he would be staying so long. Hell, he'd drifted there without even thinking his plan through.

"When did you get here?" He reached down to help her up from the floor.

"A few hours ago. I fell asleep."

"Why didn't you call Kayla?" He checked her over, a horrible feeling taking root in his gut.

Greg had never hit her before, but he'd always felt the power imbalance of their relationship and feared that one day it might take a turn. Thankfully, it didn't look like she'd been hurt. Not physically anyway.

"You know what she's like," Minnie huffed.

Yeah, Beckett knew exactly what she was like. His sister set a lot of boundaries with their mother, thinking it might teach her something. Which meant she always came to Beckett first.

"I knew you'd come home at some point." She raked a hand through her frizzy hair.

Satisfied that she didn't need to be taken to a doctor or the emergency room, Beckett dug his key out of his pocket and let them both into his apartment. "Are you going to tell me what's going on?"

Silence. After the spiel she'd given him at dinner the other night, her showing up unannounced wasn't a good sign. A lot of people could cause his mother's temper to flare up, but only one ever made her cry.

"What's he done now?" Beckett growled. "I swear to God, if he hurt you—"

"He's gone." She let out a tearful huff and shook her head, her thin lips almost disappearing as she pressed them together. "You were right, I guess. He comes and goes as he pleases."

"When are you going to stop letting him walk all over you?" Anger ripped through him like a freight train. "When he's here he stomps on everything, and he leaves you and Kayla in tears. Every goddamn time. And I'm the one who picks up the pieces."

He wanted to find that sonofabitch and tell him to stay the hell away. For good.

He'd lost count of how many times he'd been here—consoling his mother. Dreading having to tell his sister that her father was gone. Again. The man was a parental Houdini. It'd taken Kayla years to trust her fiancé. They'd known each other since they were kids, and he'd always been in love with her. But Kayla had assumed he would leave her just like her father did.

And now he was going to have to tell her it'd happened again.

"I'm sorry, Beck." Tears shimmered in his mother's eyes, her face crumpling. She looked way older than her fifty-two years—heartache etching lines into her face that shouldn't have been there. If only she could apply the take-no-bullshit attitude she had at work to her relationship with Greg.

"There's more." She hiccupped.

Ice solidified in Beckett's veins. "Tell me."

"I went out yesterday to do some grocery shopping and…" She shook her head. "My card got declined. He'd been to the bank and…and…"

Her words dissolved into a sob. He wanted to ask how she could have been so stupid to leave his name on their accounts when Greg hadn't contributed a cent in years. But they were well past that conversation now.

"How much is left?" Beckett wasn't sure he wanted to know the answer.

"Enough for a month's rent. Barely."

Jesus. All that money he'd put aside for his mother, all the blood, sweat, and tears slaving over that project so he could create a secure life for his family. Gone.

"If he ever sets foot in your house again, I swear…" Beckett's chest heaved, the cold reality freezing his blood. It was gone. All of it. "We're done, okay? This is it. I don't give a shit if he grovels until his voice gives out. He's on his own now."

His mother was nodding, tears still rolling down her cheeks. She looked deliriously tired, no doubt having stressed for hours about telling him. What the fuck was he supposed to do now?

"We can't tell Kayla yet," his mother said. "She called earlier today to ask if he was going to come to the wedding."

"Shhh." He pulled her into his arms and let her cry against his T-shirt. "We can figure it out tomorrow."

He set his kettle to boil and got his mother to make herself a cup of tea while he changed the sheets on his bed for her. No way was he letting her sleep on the couch. And tomorrow he'd go to her place and change the locks. Then they'd go to the bank and get Greg taken off her accounts.

He could fix this. There *had* to be a solution.

After his mother had drunk her tea and gone to bed, Beckett lay on the couch, staring up into the darkness. Sleep wasn't going to come, that much was clear. Not until he had a plan for how to fix the momentous fuck-up that was his life.

His mother had one month of rent. Beckett's bank account could tide her over, but she'd have to get a job to cover bills and groceries. He could sell his apartment if need be. But that was all a Band-Aid solution.

Then what?

The app wouldn't make it to market for a year, at least. And that's if they did a cut-down version of what he had planned, *and* if he had a robust team of developers helping him. Profits would take longer still to come through. If he got a job, he wouldn't have enough time to work on the startup.

As for the option of taking a loan…it was possible. He had equity in the apartment that he could borrow against, but it wouldn't be enough to cover his mum *and* get WealthHack to the next investment stage. Certainly, not the two million Lionus had promised. And the venture capitalist Beckett had met with would only get on board at this early stage by cutting the heart out of his project and leaving him with crumbs.

"Fuck," he muttered, grinding the heel of his palm into his eye.

The only way he could see to fix this problem would be to convince Lionus to support M.K. Technologies again. And that meant smoothing things over with Sherri.

The very thought of it made him want to pound his fist into something. Why now? Why, after he'd finally taken a step out of his box and discovered that there was more to life than security? It was like the universe was telling him to get back inside. To barricade the doors and go back to the old way of doing things.

Through the silence of the apartment, something rustled.

A soft, muted sound. He pushed up and padded to his bedroom door. Sobbing. Pressing his palm to the door, he sighed, wishing he knew the right words to say.

But words weren't his forte. Action was.

And that meant being with McKenna was a luxury he couldn't afford right now.

• • •

The next few days were a whirlwind for Beckett. Everything had been abandoned, except helping his mother get back on her feet. She'd resisted some of the changes—like switching out her locks and meeting with a lawyer—but this time Beckett took Kayla's advice. That meant helping Minnie face some harsh realities, instead of trying to Band-Aid the situation for her.

But the whole thing drained him completely. Caring for his family was exhausting. Emotionally. Mentally. So when he tried to throw himself into WealthHack, there was nothing left. And, after meeting with the bank and confirming they wouldn't be able to loan him enough to get the project through to seed stage, Beckett knew he only had one option left: Lionus Aldridge.

Given the older man had hung up on him earlier that week, when he'd called to see if they could work things out, the only person who would have any sway would be Sherri. No matter how he tried to figure it out, he always came back to the same solution.

Which meant he needed to talk to McKenna.

He felt like a bastard sleeping with her and then calling things off. God, he was one of *those* guys he'd hated in high school. The asshole-type he'd warned his sister away from over the years. Guilt churned in his gut like a foamy, black wave. He had no idea what to say, no idea how to break the news.

The only thing he did know was that she deserved the truth. He didn't want her finding out via some third party because he was too chickenshit to come clean with her. Beckett might not be perfect, but he wasn't a liar.

Steeling himself, he headed out of his apartment and made the short walk to her front door. Every cell in his body resisted what he was about to do, making his hand feel as though it was filled with lead as he rose it to knock.

You're doing the right thing by your family, and your future. Once you get WealthHack to market, you'll be set. Then you can start worrying about what you want. Until that point, it's about what you need.

But what did he need, really? Casting aside the money that Lionus had promised him—and the contract terms that left him in charge and in control—what *did* he need? A bed to sleep on, a roof over his head. The knowledge that his mother wouldn't have to struggle. The fundamentals.

But he'd never thought beyond that. Never wondered what lay beyond the security of basic needs, because he wasn't a guy who craved fancy holidays and fast cars. Beautiful women.

He swallowed and let his fist rap against her door. Beautiful *woman*. If he was honest with himself, there was only one person he wanted.

The door swung open and McKenna's face lit up. "Beckett! What a nice surprise. I was starting to think you were avoiding me."

He raked a hand through his hair, everything coiling up tight in preparation. Was he supposed to go inside? Or should they do it here? No, the last thing he wanted was people talking about his personal life.

"Can I come in?" he asked.

"Of course." She gestured with a wooden spoon. "I was getting dinner ready. I'm trying my hand at making a Thai red curry from scratch. I'm not the best cook, I'll be honest. But this recipe looked simple. Do you like spicy food? I've got enough for two if you haven't eaten yet."

She prattled on about the recipe, about the ingredients she'd bought fresh from the South Melbourne market, about that one time that she forgot to de-seed a chili before putting it into her meal. He let her voice wash over him for a few minutes, enjoying the tinkling highs and lows of her pitch. She spoke about everything with such excitement and passion, no matter how mundane the topic.

He could listen to that voice for the rest of his life.

Remember why you're here. Don't drag this out longer than you have to, it's not fair on either of you.

"McKenna," he said, reaching out to touch her arm. "We need to talk."

A smile quirked on her lips. It looked as though she'd been wearing lipstick, but most of it had smudged off. A stray dot of sauce had stained her chin and he had to force himself not to swipe at it with his thumb.

"That's the second time you've said that to me," she said. "I'm starting to worry I'm rubbing off on you."

Only in the best ways.

He cleared his throat. "Look, I don't know how to do this…"

Seeing her easy smile dissolve into confusion and then worry was like an icepick to his heart. She didn't deserve this.

"There have been some changes…" Shit. He'd never broken up with anyone before. But how was one supposed to do that before they were even dating? "I've had to reassess things."

Her lip quivered. "This isn't a good time to start using clichés."

"I'm still going to get back together with Sherri." Each word was like barbed wire scraping up the back of his throat, leaving him raw. Shredded. His voice wasn't even his own. He sounded jagged and robotic. Like someone else was speaking for him. "I know this isn't what you want to hear, but I need to do what's best for my family."

"Your family wants you to be with someone for the sake of money?" Her tone said she didn't believe a word of it.

"It's a long story, but—"

"I have time." She folded her arms across her chest. "And I want to hear every word of it so that I remember the exact moment I figured out that I am physically incapable of telling the good guys from the bad."

He cringed. "It's not personal, McKenna. It's nothing to do with you."

"Yes, it bloody well is." Her voice wavered. "I'm positive you're not the type of guy to sleep around for kicks. It certainly didn't feel that way the other night. *That* makes it personal."

She stared at him, her blue eyes wide and surrounded by long, soot-black lashes. Unblinking. Her small frame was dressed in all black—a fitted dress, lace tights, and chunky, flat boots. Work attire. She mustn't have been home for long.

"WealthHack is everything I've been working toward. It means my mother won't ever have to worry about making ends meet like she did when I was growing up. It means she won't have to work some crappy minimum wage job that she hates." He swallowed.

He'd never talked about his family like this to anyone. Ever. As far as people were concerned, he was just a guy who loved to create. But they were *wrong* about what he wanted to create. It wasn't an app or a lavish lifestyle or fame. It wasn't even that he wanted to change the world. He was simply a guy who wanted his bases covered. Who wanted to give his mother the one thing she'd struggled to give him.

"It's not about what I want for me," he said. "It's bigger than that."

Chapter Fifteen

McKenna didn't want to feel sympathy for Beckett. Damn him. She'd never met a guy who was so devoted to his family in her entire life. It spoke volumes about who he was as a person. But all that was overshadowed by the fact that he'd slept with her while not having any intention of sticking around.

And that spoke volumes about *her*.

Can't you get it into your head? You'll never be good enough for these guys. Gage knew it. And now Beckett knows it. So why don't you?

The drumbeat of her heart rang loud in her ears. What was wrong with her? What part of her was so broken that she couldn't read people properly? That she couldn't see the oncoming headlights of humiliation until it was too late?

His brows furrowed, an adorable crease forming between them. "I wish things were different."

She rolled her eyes. "Oh right, so now you're going to say I'm beautiful and wonderful and I deserve a man who'll treat me right. And you wish that man could be you, but it can't."

His Adam's apple bobbed, but he said nothing.

"It's easy to say that shit when you don't have to back it up. Which, ultimately, tells me it means nothing." Tears threatened and she willed herself not to cry with every ounce of control in her body. She would *not* let him see how much he'd hurt her. "But don't worry, it's not like you promised me anything to get me into bed. I don't blame you for that. I blame *me*."

"McKenna—"

"I went willingly, thinking that you showed up at my door because you felt that stupid little spark that I had. I didn't ask questions, and I ignored that voice in my head telling me to watch out. I should have listened," she charged on, letting the words erupt because if she didn't let them flow, her tears would instead. She needed to cling to anger or else she'd start to feel something else. The snap of rejection, renewed like an old wound cut open again. "But I don't blame you, really. You were clear from the start that you wanted her back and I should have known you wouldn't change your mind even though I thought we had something."

"We did have something," he said, the words low and gravelly. Not his usual calm and even tone.

"No, we didn't. Because if you really believed that, then you wouldn't be going back to her."

"I told you why it has to be this way." He raked a hand through his hair.

"Do you care about her?" She wasn't sure whether she wanted to hear him say yes or no. Each one was fraught with its own issues, and neither was a solution.

"Of course I care about her. We were supposed to be getting married." He shook his head. "It's different."

"How is it different? Do you care about me, too? Or did you sleep with me because I was there?"

The muscle in Beckett's jaw ticked. "I slept with you because I wanted to, because…I felt a connection."

So he'd felt it, too. Her chest clenched. It seemed that

even when she managed to find a decent guy, she couldn't make it work. Something always went wrong.

"But that's not enough." She looked at the floor, the hot prickles at the backs of her eyes getting stronger. Overpowering her.

He cursed under his breath. "The timing…"

"There's always something." She lifted her head, looking him straight in the eye. "You know, that night I first came to your apartment I had decided to swear off men. Temporarily, anyway."

"I didn't know that."

"Well, I had. Reason being that I make bad decisions for myself." She let out a sharp, bitter laugh. "I was determined not to let anyone else tell me I'm not good enough. But here we are."

"I am *not* telling you that." He reached out to her, but she stepped back and he dropped his arm back down by his side. "This has nothing to do with what kind of person you are."

"Aren't you going to tell me I *am* good enough, then?" she said, sarcasm weighing her words down.

"No one should have to tell you that, McKenna," he said. "You should know it."

He may as well have slapped her across the face for how badly the words stung. The entire mess had been created because she hadn't believed in herself. If she'd started working on her freelance business when she should have, then she wouldn't have needed Beckett's help to secure an important wedding. And she wouldn't have bent her own rules and slept with him, knowing that he was trying to get Sherri back.

Low self-esteem was the key ingredient in all her failings. But not for much longer.

"You know, I should thank you, Beckett." She noticed that she was still clutching the wooden spoon and headed over to the pot to stir her curry. No sense letting her dinner burn because of him. "This has been an important learning experience. And you're right, I *shouldn't* need someone to tell me I'm good enough. I'm not going to seek validation from other people anymore."

He continued to watch her, his assessing gaze fixed on her face. What was he thinking? Did he regret coming here? Would he be sorry that he walked away?

"I'm sorry that this"—she gestured to them both— "doesn't fit in with your circumstances. But I really hope you don't make her miserable so you can look after your family. Because she's a person, too. And, like me, she deserves more than some guy who's only with her for superficial reasons."

For a moment, his emotions—shock, regret, anger—were brilliantly clear in his face. It reflected in the flare of his nostrils, in the tensing of his jaw, in the flicker of his gaze to the floor and back. But, like with most things that Beckett felt, it slipped back below the surface in an instant.

"I appreciate you giving me the heads up instead of ghosting me," she said, her anger receding. Something deeper and darker had bubbled up, and she didn't want him to see it. "But I think you should leave now."

"McKenna…" He sighed, his fist clenching and releasing by his side. "I'm sorry."

No, that's *not* what she needed to hear. Because no other guy had ever made an apology for his actions, and not once had she cared. She'd always picked herself up and dusted herself off—angry, but never vulnerable. Never hollowed out and aching and so freaking *sad*.

Why now? You weren't even dating. You didn't have anything with him. One night? It's nothing.

Maybe that's why it was worse. Because it felt like they'd become friends.

"Please, just go." Her voice had taken on that strangled sound. That uneven, crackly, pre-crying sound. "I don't have anything else to say."

She turned around and promised herself that she wouldn't move until she heard the door close. The sound came without any footsteps preceding it. Like he'd vanished into thin air. Even then she counted to three before the tears fell.

. . .

After messing up his chat with McKenna, Beckett felt like a caged animal for days. He paced back and forth across his living room—unable to work, unable to move on. It was like mental quicksand. Even the few times he'd picked up his phone to call Sherri, he couldn't seem to make his fingers work.

But Kayla's rehearsal dinner was fast approaching, and he still hadn't told his family that they'd broken up. Which meant the time for fixing his mess of a life was now. He hurried down Clarendon Street toward the Wooden Llama, Sherri's café of choice. It was less than a block from her office, and if he knew his ex like he thought he did, then she'd be there at three on the dot ordering a flat white.

He got there early, bought her coffee and his. Like clockwork, she walked through the doors a moment later. Her eyes widened when they settled on him, and Beckett held out the paper cup—stamped with the café's signature llama head.

"What are you doing here?" she asked, a half smile forming on her lips.

He hadn't been sure what reaction he'd get turning up like this, but Sherri loved romantic comedies. And the guy always seemed to show up in the right place at the right time at the end of those. Given her sweet expression, it looked like his gamble had paid off.

But instead of feeling any gratitude toward his fortune, or any sense of happiness or relief at seeing her again, his stomach sank. Every cell in his body told him to get up and walk out of that café. Had he been subconsciously hoping that she'd turn him away so he could be absolved of this decision?

"I wanted to talk," he said.

God. That phrase was becoming his go-to lately…who the hell had he become?

"Wow. Okay." They took a seat at a small round table in the corner of the café.

Sherri shrugged out of her trench coat and hung it neatly on the back of her chair. She had her hair pulled back into a sleek ponytail and wore natural makeup, as she always did. Even her perfume was the same—something soft and lemon-y. Familiar.

But that familiarity only served to exacerbate the unease growing unwieldy in his stomach. The feeling of wrongness consumed him, confusing him. It occurred to him how different she and McKenna were. Both beautiful women, in their own way. But he felt none of the spark with Sherri that he did with McKenna. None of that sizzle and zing that had captured him and confounded him from the moment she'd entered his apartment to claim a wayward box of sex toys.

The memory was like a knife to his gut.

"I didn't mean to interrupt your coffee time," he said.

"Not at all." She sipped her drink, looking at him expectantly. "This is a very pleasant surprise."

This was what she'd wanted all along, for him to step outside his usual way of doing things. To surprise her. To want to talk.

It occurred to him that all that behavior had started when he'd met McKenna. In the short time they'd become friends—or however he was supposed to label it—he'd changed. Work had taken a back seat, and he'd made time for other things. A date, communication, kissing. Sex.

Incredible, mind-bending, insatiable sex.

He shook his head. Cutting ties with McKenna should

have put a stop to his thoughts about her, but instead it had the opposite result. It was like he'd unplugged something in his brain and now there was a constant stream of her filling his head.

"Did you have something you wanted to say to me, Beck?" Sherri asked softly.

What the hell was he doing? This wasn't who he was, who he was raised to be. He didn't *use* people. Leading Sherri on now would make him no better than Greg—a thief, a liar. A selfish asshole who was happy to stomp over those he should have cared about if it got him what he wanted.

"I'm sorry for how we ended things," Beckett said. He wrapped his hands around his cup, willing the warmth to unfreeze his brain. "I didn't give you the time you deserved when we were together."

She nodded, her hand reaching up to smooth her already perfect hair. "You do love your work."

"I do." He rubbed at the back of his neck. "Well, I did."

He'd treated WealthHack like it was the only thing that mattered for so long. It was the key to solving his problems, for creating security. But he knew now that security wasn't as guaranteed as he'd once thought. His mother had enough money for two years of rent, and now it was gone. Security could vanish at any time.

Just like control.

He couldn't dictate his mother's life so it would fit into his idea of an "end state." He couldn't tell her how to spend the money or whether she needed to ask for her job back or whether she should let Greg back into her life. That was him imposing his values on her.

"I told my father not to withdraw his money, for what it's worth. I know how much you had riding on it." She sighed. "But you know what parents are like."

"I do." He nodded. "And this break has given me a lot of time to think about other things."

"Like what?"

"Like how much you deserve to be with someone who truly gets you."

She tilted her head, her nose wrinkled. "I'm not sure what you're saying."

"Just that I'm sorry, and that I hope you find a man who worships the ground you walk on."

"Oh. Right." She blinked, her large brown eyes reflecting his own shock back at him. "You met someone, didn't you?"

"Yeah, I did."

"Do you love her?" Sherri's voice was tight, but she always had a good poker face when she felt she needed it. Like him.

"I don't know. It's early, but…" He paused. "It feels right."

The words should have shocked him, but voicing them aloud only confirmed what he already knew. He wanted McKenna. He wanted *more*. He wanted this perfect, emotionally messy, frighteningly satisfying thing that they had. This thing that wasn't yet formed, that couldn't be explained, that he didn't quite understand. All he knew was that she'd renewed his interest in life and it was all because she'd allowed him to be who he was.

"I don't know what to say." Sherri shook her head. "I guess I've known that something wasn't right for a long time. I kept hanging on for some reason, hoping things might change… and it looks like they did, but not how I wanted them to."

She pushed up from the table and pulled her jacket off the chair, hugging it to her chest. For a moment, he thought she might cry. But she looked as confused as he felt. Neither one of them said a word, because there wasn't really anything left to say. Their relationship had finished some time ago, only neither of them had been willing to admit it.

She walked out from behind the table and dropped her hand to his shoulder for a second, before leaving the café. Beckett stayed glued to his chair, the reality of what had happened swirling around him. When all was said and done, he couldn't go backward. That was the old Beckett, the one who relished the security of sameness.

He pulled his phone out of his pocket and swiped at the screen. If he was going to move forward, he needed a new direction. A compromise.

M.K. Technologies wasn't going to die. Not today. But perhaps playing a smaller role in WealthHack long term would mean room in his life for other things. Like the woman who'd taught him to make space.

. . .

McKenna had understood the term "butterflies in your stomach before," but she was convinced that Mothra had taken up residence in hers. Vintage horror movie references aside, she was pretty darn excited about Kayla's wedding. Even with the deep cloud of funk that had been following her around ever since Beckett broke off their relationship before it had even started.

While her love life might be as sorry as ever, business was booming. McKenna had done Kayla and her mother's makeup for the rehearsal dinner that'd taken place three nights ago. It was similar to the bridal makeup, but a little more nighttime glam since it wasn't such a formal event. And when Kayla's Instagram picture had been picked up by a local society blog, there had been questions abounding on who had done her makeup.

Since then, the contact form on McKenna's new website—the one that made her throat constrict every time she looked at it because it made her think of Beckett—had been blowing up with enquiries. She already had a three-event job booked, plus an opportunity to do some live demos at an upcoming bridal expo. She'd done that before as part of the CAM-

Ready team…but this was different. This time it would be all about *her* business.

Trying not to hyperventilate with excitement, McKenna continued disinfecting her brushes with a quick-dry spray cleaner so she could get onto Kayla's makeup. The bridesmaids were done and they looked gorgeous, if she did say so herself. The group of three women were busy taking selfies and admiring one another's final looks not far from where Kayla climbed up onto the stool.

"The girls look wonderful," she said. "I really loved the way you were able to tweak the look to make it personal for each one of them."

"All part of the job." McKenna wiped a powder brush against a piece of paper towel, swirling it around until all the product was removed. "They're unique women, so I can't take the same approach for each face."

"Did you see how many comments I got on the photo you took of me the other night?" Kayla grinned. "I made sure to tag you."

"Yes, I've had a ton of requests come in. You're my most successful face to date," McKenna said, laying the brush down.

"Maybe I should add it to my LinkedIn profile." Kayla held her hands up to her cheeks. "Mrs. Kayla Corbett, most successful face."

"It has quite a ring to it."

McKenna scanned the mass of product covering Minnie Walsh's table. It felt a little strange knowing that she was in Beckett's mother's home. It'd been difficult not to stop and stare at the photos on the mantel. But she'd stolen a quick glance when the girls had gone outside to have a break from sitting still. The photos showed a serious boy, gangly and tall, with an awful bowl cut that so many kids had back then. But his face had been strikingly handsome even from a young age. Those vivid blue eyes pierced right through her from the faded photo paper.

Even back then it looked as though his mother and sister were the cheeky ones, while he stood by them. Proud. Strong. Silent. Her throat tightened.

Stop thinking about him. The decision has been made and you didn't make the cut. End. Of. Story.

McKenna warmed a drop of primer between her fingers and then pressed it into Kayla's skin. "How are you feeling about today? Any butterflies?"

"I guess I *should* be nervous, but I feel surprisingly calm." She closed her eyes while McKenna prepped her skin. "I spent a lot of time pulling together all the details so everything would be perfect, but I had a bit of an epiphany at the rehearsal."

"Really?" McKenna pumped the foundation out onto her palette and mixed a drop of pearlescent liquid into it.

"I don't know how much Beckett has told you about our family, but my dad has never really been on the scene." She sighed. "He came back recently and I had visions of him walking me down the aisle. It's what I've wanted ever since I was a little girl. But I think I've finally accepted that he doesn't want to be part of my life."

Her heart constricted. "I'm sorry to hear that."

Kayla shook her head. "Don't be. It was one of those things I needed to learn, you know? I had to stop wishing that this absent man would come back into my life when I was already surrounded by people who love me. Beckett's giving me away."

"He'll love that." McKenna blinked back the swelling emotion. Now was not the time to get misty eyed about the guy who'd dumped her.

Taking a stippling brush, she dipped it into a contour cream and set to work carving out the hollow under Kayla's cheekbones. The effect would look amazing in photos, enhancing her already lovely bone structure.

That's right. Concentrate on the makeup, that's what you're focused on now.

But no amount of willing would stop Beckett from invading her thoughts. Every time she left her apartment she wondered if she'd see him. Every time she got into the elevator she remembered the time he'd comforted her in the dark. And every time she bought something online she double-checked her address to make sure she wasn't typing his.

Why couldn't she get it into her head that it was over?

Maybe because you've never fallen hard like that before. It felt different with him because you wanted it to go somewhere. You resisted because you knew he could hurt you…and he did.

Him leaving wasn't just a dent to her pride like with all the others. It was a dent to her soul.

"So you're going to stay at the venue until after the first dance, right?" Kayla asked.

"Yep. I'll be in the dressing room so you and the girls can come in for a touch up between the photos." She glanced critically at the area along Kayla's jawline and continued to blend with her brush. "That offer goes for your mother and the mother of the groom as well. I can do lipstick touch-ups and blot anyone who's looking a little shiny."

"Well," Kayla said with a cheeky grin. "I won't need you while the photos are being taken, and we're having the staff serve cocktails and canapes in the ballroom to keep the guests entertained. You're more than welcome to grab a drink and something to eat."

"That's very kind, but I'm driving."

She wouldn't be drinking on the job, since she'd borrowed her brother's car to get to and from Kayla's mother's house and the wedding venue. Totally worth it since Kayla was paying her double to be onsite for a few hours. But that meant no drinks for her.

"Oh, well, make sure you have something to eat. Beckett will be there after we're done with the family shots."

McKenna swallowed. "I'll be sure to say hi."

Great. The last thing she wanted was to run into Beckett and Sherri. They'd probably be acting all loved up and McKenna really didn't want to blow this important job by accidentally crying in front of everyone. Good thing she'd packed a few muesli bars and an apple into her bag. No way in hell would she be venturing out and risk bumping into them.

"Well, since he's going stag I'm sure he'd enjoy the company." Kayla had her eyes closed since McKenna had started work on her brows, but her lip twitched.

"Going stag?" The drumbeat of McKenna's heart filled her ears with an unrelenting beat. "Like alone?"

"Yeah. Since he and his fiancée broke up, she's not coming to the wedding."

Did she mean that Beckett had simply told her about the breakup that happened weeks ago? Or had something happened since?

McKenna pulled her bottom lip between her teeth and forced herself to concentrate on creating the perfect arch at Kayla's brow. A small angle brush and some dark powder created hair-like strokes, filling in gaps and ensuring they would look perfect for the camera.

Don't get excited. This doesn't change anything.

"It was rough for him. But I think it's for the best; they weren't very well suited."

"I'm sure he's very upset," McKenna said diplomatically.

"Maybe this is overstepping, but I think you two would be great together."

She raised a brow. "And I think you might be the first bride ever to play matchmaker at her own wedding."

She shrugged. "Maybe. But I'm serious."

"How do you know I don't have a boyfriend, already?"

She shot her client a mock stern look. "Now, close your eyes so I can do your eyeshadow primer."

"*Do* you have a boyfriend?"

"Well, no. I don't."

Kayla's smug silence made McKenna shake her head. Had Beckett mentioned that they'd kissed…that they done more? Surely not. He didn't seem like the kind of guy who'd kiss and tell. But Kayla's confidence rattled her.

"When did he break up with Sherri?" she asked.

"Recently. Like last week." Kayla sighed. "I'm sad for him, of course. But I think everyone saw it coming before he did."

"Right." She willed herself not to engage further but the questions in her head were like flies buzzing, getting louder and louder and one slipped out. "What about his app?"

"He's seeking alternate funding."

Her breath caught in her throat. "Really?"

"Yep. Since it's officially over, he's gone somewhere else. It'll be better that way, less personal stuff to get in the way of business." Kayla cracked an eye open. "But you should talk to him about it."

She raised a brow. "About his business?"

"About anything." The bride-to-be grinned. "I know he'd be happy to hear from you."

McKenna busied herself with inspecting the face chart she'd drawn up at Kayla's trial, pretending to concentrate on reviewing her work. But the fact was, her head and heart and stomach were on a roller-coaster ride. The soaring feeling interrupted by drastic drops as she tried to figure out what this meant.

If Beckett and Sherri were officially over, where did that leave her? Kayla could simply be meddling, having no idea that what she was suggesting was old news. All of this could mean nothing.

Or, it could mean everything.

Chapter Sixteen

Beckett stood still, his jaw hurting from smiling as the photographer took "just one more" family photo. They were standing under a gazebo ringed with jasmine bushes and the smell lifted into the air as a cold breeze rolled through. Why Kayla had chosen to get married in winter he had no idea. But he had to admit their photos with the bright yellow umbrellas against the silver and slate-toned backdrop would be striking.

Like her. His sister looked like an angel—her face was flushed with happiness and her long gown made her look like a princess. Walking her down the aisle had been one of the proudest moments of his life. It meant so much that he could take the place by her side since her father had vanished into thin air. Again.

Telling her the bad news had damn near killed him. But after she'd sobbed into his shirt, she'd shaken the tears off and had vowed to let Greg go for good. Seems like it was a theme in his family at the moment—cutting ties with the past and forging a better future.

Beckett was ready for the formality to be over. Every time

his gaze snagged on something purple, his heartbeat kicked up a notch. Kayla had made a point of telling him that McKenna would be at the wedding, but so far he hadn't seen her.

"That's it for the family portraits." The photographer motioned for Kayla and Aaron to come forward. "How about we get the bride and groom to stand over here."

The family members—which were about three times as many people on the groom's side—drifted away. A waiter with a tray of champagne cocktails was waiting outside the gazebo, ready to serve the important and senior Mr. and Mrs. Corbett. Minnie hung back, with her hands clasped together, watching on as Kayla beamed up at her new husband for the camera.

Beckett took the moment to head out of the gazebo and across the artfully manicured lawn. The blades of grass were damp underfoot, from a brief flash of rain that'd sent people scattering a few moments ago. Thankfully it had held off for most of the day, and the ceremony had been inside an old chapel on the property. But now a fine mist sprayed down from above and he hurried toward the reception building with his head bowed.

Perhaps McKenna would be in one of the rooms set aside for the bride and groom. He knew they had a spot for the ladies in the bridal party to touch up their makeup and have a breather from the three hundred-strong crowd.

Beckett strode through the front door of Patterson House. The mansion had been built in the 1800s and later turned into a heritage tourist spot and event venue for the social elite. Everything was darkly ornate, from the rich wood paneling to the patterned tile in the foyer to the gold accents and heavy chandeliers. It was opulent. Old money.

"Excuse me." He stopped the emcee, who happened to be walking past. "I need to get something from the makeup artist for Kayla. Do you know where she is?"

The stylish older man turned and pointed to a hallway off to their left. "Third door on the right."

Beckett nodded his thanks and headed in the direction the emcee had indicated. His footsteps were loud in this quiet part of the building, or maybe it was simply the blood rushing in his ears that was making all the noise. His movements felt stiff and jerky, as though he'd only just learned how to walk.

He'd wanted to go to McKenna earlier in the week, but when he'd knocked on her door she didn't answer. When he'd tried a second time, he could have sworn he'd heard footsteps but no one came. That's when he remembered that he had the perfect plan all along. McKenna's four-point plan.

Step one: Make contact. He'd texted and tried to call, but those attempts, too, had gone unanswered.

Since Beckett had recently learned that one needed to be adaptable when plans change, he had decided to skip straight to step two. A face-to-face meeting. And if she wasn't going to answer her front door, then he would go to where a lock wouldn't stand in his way.

He sucked in a breath and smoothed his hands down the front of his tuxedo before he raised his hand to knock. Once. Twice.

The door swung open and McKenna's smiling face turned to shocked stone when she saw it was him. "Beckett. Hi."

"Hi, McKenna." Seeing her was enough to ease the ache in his chest that had grown each day they'd been separated by his stupidity. "I've been practicing my return greetings."

"No grunting. Very well done." A shy smile started to blossom, but she pressed her lips into a line as though remembering that she was supposed to be angry with him. "What can I do for you?"

"Would it sound horribly repetitive if I said we need to talk, again?"

She peered out of the room and looked down the hallway.

"I don't know if this is the best time. I'm working."

"I have permission from the bride. Well, not permission so much as a direct order."

She tucked a strand of hair behind her ear and sucked in a breath. "Okay, fine. But the second anyone else comes in, you'll need to leave."

He pressed a hand to his chest. "I solemnly promise not to get in the way of your makeup magic."

She shut the door behind them and clasped her hands in front of her. Like the last time he'd seen her, she was dressed in black from head to toe. It made her purple hair and hot-pink lipstick look neon against the dark canvas. When she blinked, little flashes of silver beckoned him closer. God, she was so beautiful.

"What do you want to talk about?" she asked. She shifted from one booted foot to the other, her breath choppy and shallow. "Do I need to sit?"

"Well, the plan only says that I need a face-to-face meeting, it didn't mention whether it should be sitting or standing." He pulled out the printed email and showed it to her. "See, I'm up to step two."

"You skipped step one," she said. It was hard to tell whether she was playing along because she wanted to talk to him. Her usual spark was hiding behind an impassive, neutral expression that told him absolutely nothing.

"I *attempted* step one." He raked a hand through his hair, trying to remember all the things he'd planned to say. But words vanished around her, because they didn't feel important. The thunderous beating in his chest, the fire burning in his blood, the itch in his palms that compelled him to reach out to her—*those* were important. "So, according to this plan, step three is 'give her a chance to have her say.' Apparently, it will be natural for me to want to defend myself but this is her time to air her concerns."

"I wrote that, huh?" She studied him, her arms folded across her chest. The defensive position wasn't a great sign, but there was a softening in her face. A slight dimple in her cheek that hinted a smile might be close. "Too bad you're using it on the wrong girl."

"I'm not, McKenna. The only thing that's wrong about this situation is that I didn't figure it out sooner." He dropped the piece of paper onto the desk that had her brushes neatly laid out.

"Figure out what?" Her eyes tracked him as he moved forward, darting back and forth as if she were assessing her risk. Assessing whether she should run.

This was the bit he couldn't seem to work out. The right words to say, ones that would adequately express all the new and confusing things he felt. His insides were tangled up, like a bunch of wires. But that didn't sound right. His heart was like a sledgehammer pounding through a wall. But that wasn't right, either.

He wanted to say something profound and important and insightful. Something that would show her he regretted every moment that he'd been running in the wrong direction. Every second he'd wasted chasing after the wrong thing in life, hurting her in the process.

"I care about you," he said eventually. "I care about you more than I feel is logical."

Her lip quivered. "You care about me? How? In what way? More than you feel is logical...what does that even mean?"

"It means I don't understand it. But I feel it." He swallowed against the tightness in his throat. "I don't have flowery descriptions, but I know not being with you made me more miserable than anything else I've ever experienced."

"Really?" Her eyes shimmered as she looked up, meeting his gaze head-on in a way that made him feel like he'd been struck by lightning. The power of it was like a sign. *This* was where he belonged. With her. Talking to her. Feeling out of his comfort zone with her.

"That day you knocked on my door changed everything," he said. "You changed me."

• • •

McKenna was worried about the very real possibility of her fainting for a second time in Beckett's presence. This time she didn't need the sight of blood, the feeling of it leaving her head was reason enough. Because she wanted so hard to believe he was the right man for her—that he *did* care for her in a way that was more than friendship. That they were more than people who waved in the hallway. Who said hello in the mailroom.

She wanted it all with Beckett—all the things she'd dared not wish for because she thought she'd never be good enough. But he was the one who'd told her she didn't need anyone's validation to know that. Not her boss's, not her family's.

Not even his.

"You've changed me, too," she said. "I'm not scared to aim high anymore. I'm not afraid to go after what I deserve instead of settling."

Heat simmered in his blue gaze. Against the stark black-and-white tux, they gleamed like jewels. A perfect marriage of turquoise and teal. Vibrant. Intense. But it was the feeling behind them that got her this time. He'd lost his wall, that impenetrable mask that had always kept her at arm's length. Now emotion rolled over his face like clouds blowing on the wind. He was letting her see everything. Laying himself bare.

"Good." He nodded. "I want you to have it all."

"So you broke things off for good?" she asked after a heartbeat or two. She had to know, because this time she wouldn't deal with the uncertainty. The doubt.

"I did."

"What about your business?"

"I went back to the venture capital firm and I agreed to their conditions." He nodded slowly, as though he were still coming to terms with his decision. "I've agreed to some of the changes they want, negotiated a few more."

"And their cut?"

"The same as they offered me before."

"But that's not what you wanted?" Despite it all, she felt bad knowing how much power he'd given up. Whereas Lionus Aldridge would have given him free reign, working with a venture capital firm meant being held to constraints. Conditions. Losing control.

"No, but I'll make it work. It's a compromise, but it means that I can have the other things I want." He reached for her hand, his grip warm and secure. "It means I get to be here, asking you to forgive me for being a blind idiot."

"Technically, you haven't asked yet," she said, smirking.

"McKenna Prescott, will you forgive me for being so stupid and rigid that I almost threw away what will surely be the very best thing in my life?"

His words were like a strike to her heart. "Wow," she breathed. "When you do say something, it's worth the wait."

"Well?"

"I forgive you." She stepped closer and pressed her palms to his chest, breathing in the scent of rain on his hair and the faded cologne on his skin. "See, told you the plan would work."

"I have one more step." He brought his lips down to hers in a probing kiss, soft and yet desperately raw. Her fists curled into his shirt, tugging him closer. "Step four."

"Make a commitment," she whispered, remembering the hollowed-out feeling plaguing her as she'd typed that email.

If only she'd known it would bring him back to her. "It needs to be concrete."

"I promise that I'll do everything to make you feel like you're my top priority at all times. I promise to spend time with you, to communicate with you, and to always accept your mail, even if it's really weird."

A laugh burst forth, and she shook her head. "Don't you knock Mr. Whopper. He's the reason we're together now."

"Tell him he's been replaced." Beckett's teeth nipped at her ear. "You've traded him in for the real thing."

Beckett backed her up against the door, his hips pinning her.

"Don't mess up my makeup," she said. "I'm supposed to look professional."

He planted a hand by her head, bringing his lips down to her neck. "There's no makeup here."

She moaned and let her head fall back against the door while he feasted on her. She couldn't wait for the wedding to be over, so they could finish what he'd started. Something told her that she wouldn't mind Beckett grunting in *that* scenario.

As he popped the buttons on her blouse, his lips chasing her exposed skin, McKenna sighed. The sounds of the old building came alive in their silence, broken only by his moan as his lips reached the edge of her bra. Sure, it wasn't a word but she didn't think she'd ever get tired of hearing it.

"Maybe we should come up with a new story on how we met," she said, her eyes flittering shut as his palm cupped her breast. "You know, in case we do need to explain it to your family. Or mine. Oh God, what if my mother—"

"Shhh." He placed a finger over her lips. "We've got twenty minutes, max. Let's not waste it talking."

She could be quiet for now. But the second she got Beckett back to her place, she was going to scream every word she knew, starting with *yes*.

Epilogue

Six months later…

"You're not supposed to see me in my dress before the ceremony." McKenna's voice floated through the closed door.

Beckett grinned. It wasn't him seeing her in the dress that she should be worried about. It was more trying to avoid his attempts to get her *out* of the dress.

"Pretty sure that's only for the bride and groom," he replied. "And doesn't extend to the bridesmaid and her plus one."

The door opened a fraction and McKenna stuck her head out. For once, her makeup was subdued. None of her usual fringy eyelashes or glitter, which apparently had been at the order of the bride. But he liked her all ways—made up, au natural, and everything in between.

"All right, troublemaker. What do you want?" She looked him up and down, nodding in approval. He'd wanted a basic black suit but McKenna had talked him into a gray with baby-blue pinstripes. "Looking good, by the way. I can't believe you wanted to get *another* black suit."

"Lucky I have you to talk me out of any potentially boring decisions," he said drily. "Now come out here."

"Please don't tell me we have to talk again," she teased. "All you want to do is *yap, yap, yap*." She made a talking motion with her hands. "I can't stand it."

"Don't make me gag you, again," he growled as she stepped out of the bridesmaids' room. "I had entirely too much fun listening to you try to talk with all that silk in your mouth."

"Mr. Walsh," she admonished in a mock serious tone. "I am a *lady*. Here you are, trying to corrupt my sensibilities."

"Sensibilities?" He pulled her to him and she squeaked, her gaze darting down the hall to see if anyone was coming. "I don't remember you being too sensible when you let me get into your skirt at my sister's wedding."

"Hoping for a repeat?" She raised a brow, but her eyes were wide. Her cheeks flushed. She wanted this as much as he did.

"Not hoping." He led them farther into the hallway, toward an alcove he'd spotted that had a rather dense-looking plant. "Planning."

She smacked his arm. "And here I was thinking that you were a nice, upstanding gentleman who was going to make an honest woman of me one day."

He pulled them into the alcove and cupped her face with his hands. "I can't wait, McKenna."

"I can't wait, either." The cheeky smile softened and she tipped her face up to his. "I love you."

Her eyes widened as the words popped out. They'd been dancing around it for some time, the urge to say those three little words sitting ever-present in the back of his throat. But they'd taken things slow, getting to know one another.

Last week she'd moved into his apartment when her

lease had ended. It wasn't a big change, since she slept over often. But making it official had been like a great big check mark next to their relationship. Sacrificing control with his business to have her in his life had been the best decision he'd ever made.

"I love you, too," he said.

He pulled her deeper into the alcove to punish that beautiful mouth of hers. "You sure we can't ditch this thing and head back to the room?"

"I don't think Isla would be too happy about that," McKenna murmured.

Beckett's thumbs grazed her temples as he held her in place, coaxing her lips open for a deep kiss. "You know, we could make this our thing."

"Getting naughty at other people's weddings?" She giggled.

"And hopefully at ours one day." He rested his forehead against hers. "But I'll wait until after the ceremony then, I promise."

"Shhh." She pressed a fingertip to his mouth, joy filtering through her body at the thought of their future. It seemed so bright. So sparkling. It was everything she'd been looking for.

His lips curved into a wicked grin as he lowered his head to hers, capturing her mouth and pinning her to the wall. For the first time in her life, McKenna was totally happy not to be talking.

Acknowledgments

My makeup journey has been full of inspiration from the industry greats—Kevyn Aucoin, Bobbi Brown, Pat McGrath, and the creators of MAC: Frank Toskan and Frank Angelo. Your artistry and wisdom has opened me up to a vibrant and colorful world.

Thanks must go to my mother, for teaching me about makeup in my early years, for always being happy to talk about lipstick, and for supporting my decision to go to makeup school.

Thank you to all the women who have lent their faces over the years so I could hone my skills. A special thank you to my sister, Sami, who always sat patiently through makeup applications whenever I felt the urge to create.

Huge thanks to the team at Entangled, especially to Alycia Tornetta and Liz Pelletier, for supporting my stories and giving them such a wonderful home.

And to my incredible agent, Jill Marsal, thanks for putting all my deadlines into a spreadsheet so we could figure out when on earth I was going to write all these books.

As always, I have to mention the love and support of my husband. Thank you for being my biggest cheerleader and for your unflinching belief that I can do anything no matter how crazy my schedule gets.

About the Author

Stefanie London is the *USA TODAY* bestselling author of more than ten contemporary romances with humor, heat, and heart.

Growing up, Stefanie came from a family of women who loved to read. Thus, it was no surprise she was the sort of student who would read her English books before the semester started. After sneaking several literature subjects into her "very practical" business degree, she got a job in communications. When writing emails and newsletters didn't fulfill her creative urges, she turned to fiction and was finally able to write the stories that kept her mind busy at night.

Originally from Australia, she now lives in Toronto with her very own hero and is currently in the process of doing her best to travel the world. She frequently indulges in her passions for good coffee, lipstick, romance novels, and zombie movies.

Find love in unexpected places with these satisfying Lovestruck reads...

WRAPPED UP IN YOU
a novel by Cyn D. Blackburn

For Officer Justin Weaver, Christmas is the most hideous time of the year. To improve his "holiday cheer," he's been put on Officer Kringle duty, collecting toys for the Ho-Ho-Patrol. Worse, it comes with an elf—his little sister's gorgeous best friend—but Lilly Maddox isn't so little anymore. Now that they're trapped in his squad car, avoiding her just got a lot more complicated...

THE ATTRACTION EQUATION
a *Lover Undercover* novel by Kadie Scott

FBI agent Max Carter's life isn't conducive to relationships—not that it's stopping his matchmaking mama. To avoid yet another set-up, he announces he has a girlfriend. And now he's required to bring her to Christmas dinner. Good thing he caught his sexy neighbor down the hall sneaking a dog into their decidedly "no pets" building, because she's *exactly* the woman for the job...

BRIDESMAID BLUES
a *Wedding Favors* novel by Boone Brux

Maid-of-Honor Dani Brown can handle anything that comes her way when it comes to her best friend's wedding. That is, until the bride asks for a huge favor—Dani needs to distract the best man, Jamie Kingsland...who happens to be Dani's ex. Even though Jamie knows he broke Dani's heart last year, she's being way too nice. And it scares him. Something is up with his favorite bridesmaid, and he's determined to find out what.

Made in the USA
Coppell, TX
01 July 2020